Praise for Benatar novels reissued by Welbeck

WISH HER SAFE AT HOME

'A masterpiece...matchlessly clever...wholly original.'
*John Carey*

'With this marvellous book, character and poetry return to the English novel... Rachel is one of the great English female characters, like the Wife of Bath or Flora Finching: both an individual and a species.'
*Times Literary Supplement*

RECOVERY

'A haunting and highly enjoyable love story.'
*Prunella Scales*

'A beguiling masterclass in modern fiction. Tension inexorably builds toward a gripping conclusion...the sort of book you start reading especially slowly as the final pages arrive.'
*James O'Brien, LBC Radio*

THE MAN ON THE BRIDGE

'Great understanding and depth of feeling.'
*New Statesman*

'Handles tricky material with conviction and assurance.'
*Guardian*

LETTERS FOR A SPY

'A thrilling romantic adventure, with superior characterization
and an acute eye for detail.'
*Henry Fitzherbert, Sunday Express*


WHEN I WAS OTHERWISE

'An intriguing, funny, sometimes exciting and, finally, sad story;
the elegant idiosyncrasy of the author's viewpoint, which made
*Wish Her Safe at Home* so enjoyably inventive without
discarding a carefully controlled narrative, here creates a moving
story from what might first appear to be the elements of a
black farce.'
*Christopher Hawtree, Literary Review*

'This book is remarkably convincing... One's first reaction on
finishing the novel is "Goodness, how sad!" One's second is
"Goodness, how funny!"
*Francis King, Spectator*

'Sparkling social comedy... the comparisons that come to mind
are Ayckbourn's plays and Austen's minor characters.'
*Gillian Carey*

*

Three other reissues in the pipeline:

Such Men are Dangerous
Father of the Man
The Golden Voyage of Samson Groves

# Stephen Benatar

# A Christmas Story

16.12.09

For Matthew

Stephen Benatar.

Welbeck Press

First published by the Welbeck Press, December 2009

Welbeck Press
4 Parsifal Road
London NW6 1UH
Telephone: 020 7433 8084

ISBN: 978-0-9554757-6-4

Cover design and photograph: John Murphy

Printed by:
Broadfield Press Limited
75 Broadfield Lane, London NW1 9YS
Telephone: 020 7482 5282

*A Christmas Story* is for Anthony, who many years ago – so many that I have now, shamefully, forgotten his surname – provided me with the original idea, along with much invaluable help in its plotting. Thank you, Anthony. Hope you're pleased with the result and that you and Howard are well and happy and thriving.

And it is also for John Murphy…whose fingerprints are all over it – in the same way, indeed, that these are all over my life – and for whose care and concern I shall always feel immensely grateful.

Lastly, it is dedicated to my grandchildren – but in no particular order, as they always say on *The X Factor* – :

Gabriel and Marguerite
Beatrice, Stella and Bart
William, Flora, Rose and Barnaby
Sam, Katherine and Alice.

# 1

I was being spied on.

I'd simply been sitting on my usual bench – killing time and minding my own business.

But someone was spying on me. Someone had left an envelope. It lay there in my lap. Face-up. It could have fallen out of heaven…or out of the plane tree overhead. Yet this was December and the tree was leafless. So who could have been hiding there? Houdini?

And, anyway, why should a word like *spying* ever have crossed my mind? Oh, for Pete's sake, get a grip!

"Mr Richard Semple. Victoria Embankment. Special Delivery."

Very special delivery! The pavement thereabouts was empty. No running feet, no furtive glances. There'd been no bicycle or skateboard. No slamming of car doors. What's more, I hadn't been taking a swig or having a kip. My eyes hadn't been closed. I felt certain of these things.

Besides, who in the world – apart from Social Security – would ever have known me as anything but Dick? *Richard* Semple, indeed! *Mr* Richard Semple!

The envelope was vellum. Written in high style, with a fountain pen or quill. Broad nib, black ink, authoritative. But probably more friendly than official. I sat studying it. Took my time. Felt that, compared to the possibility of what it might contain, whatever it did contain was bound to be a letdown. A letdown – even if it held a five-pound note!

No, too stiff for just a banknote. I stretched the fantasy a little further. Ten pounds now – or maybe twenty – taped inside a Christmas card.

Oh, come on, man. Stop dreaming! Do you *still* believe in Santa Claus?

The letter was deckle-edged. It came from somebody signing himself as Odin.

"Dear Semple, could you pop into my office for a word or two? A drink or two? Cigar or two? I shall look very much forward to seeing you, old chap."

Goodness me! And they say that there's no God!

So, even without the presence of a banknote, I wasn't disappointed. I knew the writer was a gentleman. I liked his informality: particularly, the easy way he said 'or two'.

Well, what could I lose? The office was in Park Lane. I struggled to my feet and tightened the rope around my overcoat. I ran a hand through hair and straggly beard. Noticed how matted my fingerless grey gloves were. Then noticed something more remarkable.

Two birds were watching from a nearby roof. Not simply watching but s*taring*, their gazes trained on me like surveillance cameras.

Ridiculous.

Still, the moment they knew I'd spotted them, it was as though someone had cried out, "Police!" I looked up towards those cameras and saw the clean-cut flap of wings. And off they flew beneath the darkening sky.

I thought at first they might be eagles, or even vultures. Which shows how much the booze had affected me. They weren't birds of prey; merely common or garden ravens. Nothing interesting. But very black. And even on a dreary morning such as this, even from a distance, you could see their plumage gleam.

They should have been beautiful; and in a way they were; but somehow they were also... What?

Ominous.

# 2

No 12 Park Lane was unique: all spires, turrets and windows of green stained glass. Gargoyles, each with only one eye. Balcony of black wrought iron, fashioned like a pair of wings – wings so fine you felt a decent breeze could stir them into life. They'd bear away the building.

Engraved in stone over the doorway was an inscription: 'By the Stars, in the Light, find the Source, use your Might.' I examined it suspiciously. My mood wasn't so upbeat any longer. It's a fair walk from the Embankment. I wondered what I was doing here.

A doorman came out. (How had he known about my presence?) Grudgingly, I showed him the letter.

He smiled and admitted me. Said he'd have to put a band around my wrist. What nonsense!

"Sorry, sir. It's a matter of security."

"Security, my foot!"

But I hadn't come this far to be fobbed off.

And, besides, I'd been distracted. Some glamour-puss was speaking into a phone. Her eyes glittered beneath spiky lashes. Her voice was surprisingly soft. "Good morning," she was cooing. "E.Y. Enterprises. How may I help you?"

"What's E.Y. Enterprises?" I asked the doorman, gruffly.

"Why, sir, that's us! You're standing in our head office." Hardly illuminating but at least he was polite; I wasn't much used to politeness.

The security band was like the sort they make you wear in hospitals, except that this one wasn't flesh-coloured. It was pale green.

"Now, sir, if you'd like to take the lift – and you'll be sure, won't you, to press the button for the penthouse? – one of Lord Odin's aides will be awaiting you."

*Lord* Odin?

I got him to repeat it. I thought it might be wooziness. Or earwax.

3

But it wasn't. Not either of those things. Holy Moses! Did this mean that I was visiting the gentry?

*

"Ah, old chap! Yes, they told me you were on your way. Longspoon, why haven't you taken Mr Semple's coat and carrier bags?"

It hadn't been for want of trying. Despite the radiators – and the open fireplace, with its cheerfully crackling logs – I'd resolutely fought to hold onto my possessions.

"Of *course*! That's fine. Not daunted by the stubbornness of secretaries! I like that. Nor by the sumptuousness of your surroundings. Oh, hallelujah! If there's one thing I can't stand it's people being impressed by the numbers of one's staff or the cost of one's furniture."

He laughed.

Lord Odin appeared to be in his forties, so handsome, tall and lean you might have called him godlike. He wore a charcoal pinstriped suit, crisp white shirt and red silk tie. He sported an eye-patch. A livid scar ran round his neck. But even such details as these enhanced his aura of distinction.

His skin was lightly bronzed, his coal-black hair in striking contrast to his deep blue eyes.

No. Deep blue *eye*.

"And now, my dear Semple, sit down and tell me what you'd like to drink. I think you'll find this chair quite comfortable. It ought to be, if price is anything to go by!"

I asked him – while trying not to show the very depth of my longing – whether I might have a shot of Scotch. Secretary Longspoon came gliding over with a brimming glass. Just like the glamour-puss downstairs, she spoke with a softly cooing voice.

"Ginger ale, Mr Semple? Or soda, Mr Semple? And, Mr Semple, would you like some ice?"

"You're a good egg, my dear. But this is absolutely fine."

And in all honesty there wouldn't have been much room for anything else. (Not that I was complaining – oh, not at all!)

"Sensible fellow," said Lord Odin. "I can see you know what's what. Pointless, then, my trying to disguise that this is the finest whisky in existence – and undeniably, of course, the most expensive. Well, cheers, my worthy Richard! Always may you prosper as you do today! Oh…and naturally you're going to sample one of these superlative Havanas?"

Well, I ask you. The man was charismatic. How could I fail to be enchanted?

Surely Merlin himself would have fallen beneath his spell.

# 3

"Exceedingly generous," I murmured.

Lord Odin held up his hand.

"Oh, exceedingly generous, pooh! I get so bored with hearing that. For even if I *am* exceedingly generous, where does it ever get me?"

I felt surprised.

"No, Richard. I'll tell you something. Do you know whom in this world I'd most like to switch places with, if only it were possible?" He paused, whilst watching me shake my head. "*You*," he smiled.

I don't know what I'd been expecting. But not that. Most certainly not that.

"The life of the open road!" he declared. "The joy of being a slave to no one! Untrammelled by possessions!"

By this time he was tilted back in his swivel chair, ankles neatly crossed upon the desk; shoes black and gleaming and pristine-soled. (Mine were held together by gaffer tape and had lino for insoles, designed to keep the wet out.) His hands were clasped composedly behind his head, a snazzy gold wristwatch uncovered by a drawn-back cuff.

"Yes, how I envy you," he said.

I still had difficulty in understanding.

He added: "And especially at this time of year."

"Winter?" I asked.

"December," he replied.

A further puzzle, then. Why should his lordship's envy be aroused more in December than in July? From the looks of him, he liked to have a tan.

"Christmas," he explained. "You see, I have a small confession to make. I don't much care for Christmas."

Well, here at last was something which I *could* relate to. "Then that makes two of us," I said.

He looked at me with raised eyebrows.

"No, my dear friend, I can't believe that. Everybody loves Christmas."

"Everybody, sir, bar one. I haven't loved Christmas for a very long time."

"*Really*?" He scrutinized my face, almost dazzling me with that fiercely bright eye of his. "And here was I feeling so terribly ashamed and guilty. Well, well! What a tonic you are – so upright, so completely fearless! You'll even tell me next you don't much care for children?"

This last bit was accompanied by a shy laugh and could easily have been a joke. But somehow I knew that it wasn't. Well, how very flattering, I thought, that he should have chosen *me* to confide in! Him, a nobleman, now baring his troubled soul to somebody like myself – a hobo. I drew deeply on my cigar and enjoyed its strangely sweet aroma. And knowing I could give him the answer he wanted only added to my pleasure.

"Children? Can't stand 'em," I said.

And as I spoke I was remembering a particularly foul-mouthed trio that had taunted me recently in the park. They'd filled plastic bottles from the pond and drenched me in its rank water. Moreover, the instant before doing this, one of the cheeky blighters had shouted, "Get yourself a wash, mister! Is that a tide mark round your neck?"

So now I gave a brief but uncontrollable shiver. "Proper little horrors!"

"Honestly?" he asked. "Honestly?" It was practically a whisper – reverential – we might have been in church. I swear I saw his lips tremble. "But, no, I'm sure you're just being kind? Everybody loves children."

"You said everybody loved Christmas."

"Yes, but I mean... Oh, pinch me, someone! I think I must be dreaming."

*

It was almost as if 'someone' – called on like this – had instantly obeyed his summons; Lord Odin immediately changed the subject.

"Now, old fellow, you must have another drink." He swung his feet down from the desk and came to see I got a good one. "Truly, a man after my own heart," he affirmed.

I mumbled my thanks. Then remembered my manners and tagged on his name and title – albeit self-consciously.

Which gave him some amusement.

"Oh...'Lord Odin'. What a mouthful! No, no, Richard, don't even try it. Anyway – best friends abbreviate. I know!" he exclaimed. "I'll call you Rich! And you must call me Lord. How's that for an idea?"

To receive so great an honour! I could scarcely credit it. Even the cigar seemed to glow in celebration. (He himself wasn't smoking; nor, in fact, drinking. But he watched appreciatively as the cigar plumes weaved themselves about my head.) "But, no, Rich – please – no gulpy struggles to reply. I know just how it is: one gets all clogged up; one's insides go all warm and mushy!" He smiled, in tender understanding.

"And now," he said, "since we've grown to be such good friends I'm sure that you're going to sympathize with *me*, when I mention one or two of my own little problems."

"*Your* problems...Lord?"

"Yes, Rich. Such are the sad demands of trying to make a living. And, as you can see, I haven't found it easy."

Ah! So now we were talking business? Despite my being where I was, right there in the head office of the head office, I still had no clue as to the possible function of E.Y. Enterprises. I did my best to stay attentive and to look astute.

"What a fine jest!" he said. "Not only can I not escape Christmas – as *some* people can, such lucky devils – but, would

7

you believe it, I'm even obliged to find a Santa Claus for some of this country's biggest department stores? I mean, one Santa Claus *each*! Oh, misery me and lack-a-day!"

He had been restlessly pacing the room but now he stopped for a minute and put the heel of each hand to the sides of his forehead. It was a gesture both of humorous despair and eloquent self-mockery.

"And the worst part is: I can find so few intelligent people who are willing to help me out. In fact – at this present time – nary a one."

I puffed at my cigar and looked to it for inspiration.

"Well, I don't see that, Lord. I mean... Well, for a start, you've got *me* here, haven't you?"

There was another pause. Lord Odin looked utterly incredulous. A moment ago he had been mournful; practically suicidal. Now there were signs of renewed hopefulness. A tentative yet burgeoning joy.

He gazed at me expectantly.

"Can't *I* help you out?" I said.


# 4


But sweet heavens! How had it come about? That whole situation had turned scary.

*Nightmarish.*

I stood outside Hagalaz & Son in Oxford Street. I didn't want to go in. I had a fear of large public buildings, of being hemmed in by crowds and of seeing – one after another – a thousand people shy away from me.

Now I also had a fear of what would happen when I reached the top.

However, I gave myself a pep talk on the pavement, then finally followed a customer through that vast, imposing entranceway. But after that – oh, God! – I stood transfixed, like some small woodland animal caught in the glare of a headlamp. And at the same time I was overwhelmed by a tidal wave of warmth and heady perfumed air. Glamorous women behind counters, as if synchronized, all turned to smile at me alluringly.

Yet I must have imagined it. For suddenly I was pushed back against the heavy glass door by a shaven-headed thug in uniform. His stubby fingers were splayed across my chest.

I might have been taller than him but he was the one with all the strength.

"Off with you, Sunshine! We don't want any of your sort here!"

Outside again. Him along with myself. Scattered pedestrians skirted around us, some pushing hurriedly into the store, dragging their children after them and throwing us nervous glances; others stopping to look back from further up the pavement.

But of course! Of course! I had in my pocket a letter of introduction to Mr Scolo...oh, to Mr Scolo-Thingumajig, the owner!

Yet as I reached for this the security guard's hand whipped across and grabbed my arm. Twisted it behind my back and propelled me away from the entrance, his every whispered word a poisoned droplet in my ear.

"No, none of that, Sunshine! You keep yourself to yourself, before we need to call the police and have you up on a charge of grievous bodily harm! But who wants policemen and unpleasantness – eh, Sonny Jim? So why not save us all a bit of bother and take a friendly tip and just *push off!*"

We were almost at the kerb. He started cautiously to move away. I felt dazed, confused; cast out, defeated. A blur of red buses sped by. "What if...?" I thought. "What if...?"

But that was only very fleeting. I hadn't got the nerve. No way.

I steeled myself and turned back towards the store; towards my blank-eyed bovver boy.

And this time I was more prepared. I advanced on him, brandishing my letter of authorization. Again, a vellum envelope. Flap unsealed. Black, attention-grabbing script.

Here, then, was my *open sesame!*

Yet wouldn't you know it? He made to snatch the envelope. I tenaciously held on, shielding it against me, with my back towards him. Heavens above – this was practically basketball! With arms outstretched and just beyond the reach of my opponent, I managed to pull the letter from its envelope, and even to unfold it. He eventually lowered his heels to the pavement, relaxed his grip upon my shoulder, reluctantly began to read.

He mouthed each word aloud. His face – like a plate of semolina having strawberry jam gradually stirred in – grew more and more flushed.

A small enough victory, maybe. Yet satisfying. It gave my confidence a boost.

But I had forgotten all those clockwork and synthetic sirens: still armed with their perfume bottles and their sprayed-on smiles, still commanding the straits beside the doors.

And the place looked so alarmingly busy. Swarming! I had to wonder what in God's name was drawing me further in. "Why do I *need* to be admitted to this hell?"

## 5

As we left Personnel, Mrs Mangosteen, plump and slightly breathless, her complexion downy as a ripening peach, walked companionably at my side. She didn't seem at all put off by me – neither by my appearance nor by my smell. Instead, she appeared motherly; even wore the same comforting fragrance as my own mother used to: Lily of the Valley. "Now, Mr Semple, don't you lose those luncheon vouchers! You'll go hungry without them!" She continued to chat pleasantly as she conducted me back to the lift and down to the fifth floor. (Administration was located on the sixth and seventh.)

We emerged directly into Toys. Angels floated from the ceiling, and each held a bugle to his lips – on which, perhaps, to blow some joyous fanfare. Up on the walls were paintings of choristers bearing lanterns. Festoons of holly hung between the

10

pillars.

And, as well as colour, there was movement: a constant swirl of youngsters who possibly believed they had just entered paradise. *Oh please, I want, must have, I'll never ask for anything again!*

Delirious children. Harassed parents. Hardly a pleasant scene...and yet there was something about it which gave me a real buzz. (Or was it an energy passing straight into me from my surroundings; I mean, out of the toys themselves?) That was ridiculous, I knew, but I was aware of a steady tingle, reminding me of something I must have experienced only recently. I couldn't pin down what.

But perhaps it was solely due to the niceness of Mrs Mangosteen, that buzz I was getting. She led me to the man who was in charge of the department. "Oh, I'm leaving you in such excellent hands!" she informed me. "Mr Daglock will take you so very tenderly beneath his wing! Won't you, Mr Daglock?"

"Don't worry, Mrs Mangosteen. I shall keep a most vigilant eye upon him at all times." This was accompanied by a sharp click of the heels, which seemed to reassure her in some way. "Yes, at *all* times," he repeated.

She smiled and gave my arm a squeeze. I felt a little sad to see her walk away.

But Mr Daglock also appeared friendly; showed me the changing room, the canteen, lavatories and fire exits – told me where the staff entrance was – made me feel at home.

That is, he appeared friendly towards *me*. His quick eyes were always on the move, however. The hairs in his nostrils quivered like a centipede's antennae. And all at once a whippet of anger was unleashed against some deeply unfortunate salesman. Apparently, this poor fellow had sold a toy straight off a display stand, when he should have sent to the stockroom for a replica. "Numbskull! Imbecile! *Never* again! Do you understand me? *Never* again!"

But this outburst had an odd element of comedy about it. Put me in mind of some Victorian school story. It was like an ill-behaved pupil being punished by his red-faced headmaster. Perhaps being threatened with the cane.

Yet why should I chuckle over someone getting into trouble?

Anyway, I then had to change into my costume: red velour and white trim. Hat with pompom. Shiny black belt. Leather boots. First smart clobber I'd possessed in years.

Or smart, at least, until I put it on. The thing was, I'd merely removed my overcoat; wasn't going to take anything else off. Therefore I felt a bit trussed up. Hardly surprising. But, annoyingly, when I expanded to draw breath, three of the silly buttons tore away from the jacket and shot off into no doubt distant places. And when I had to sit to pull my boots on...well, blow me if those pesky trousers didn't split in much the same mortifying fashion! Finally, I reached up to fix my hat – and, lo and behold, the seams at either armpit made a similar (maybe identical) loud ripping sound.

Well, whose fault was this? To me it seemed obvious. Cheap material! Shoddy workmanship!

Though – I do have to admit it – physically, I felt a lot more comfortable.

Yet I wasn't sure about the beard. Superfluous. In the end I discarded it in the goods lift, whilst going back to the fifth floor. I'd kept my overcoat, of course, but left my old shoes in the changing room.

And if anybody wanted them – well, they would be welcome! I intended never to relinquish these new ones. Intended to hang on to them forever. Aye, forever and a day!

*These boots are made for walking and that's just what they'll do.*

Yet all the same I wasn't really in any mood to sing about it. Not since I knew that at any moment Mr Daglock might come leaping forth from his place of concealment. To ambush me, and to inspect. *I* certainly didn't want to be threatened with the cane!

And I was absolutely right about the ambush.

But I was totally wrong about the inspection. "Oh, splendid," he remarked. "Perfectly splendid."

So it appeared he hadn't noticed the rips. Nor the missing buttons. But surely, with those darting eyes of his (as well as his thin, quivering nostrils) he couldn't, could *not*, have been short-sighted?

No. For the moment, he must merely have been abstracted.

"Right, then. Off we go. Around the back, naturally."

Santa's Christmas Grotto was in one of the farther corners of the huge department. (Santa's Castle of Snow stood facing it, about ten yards away – "But just forget about that, it needn't concern you, Semple. Not in the slightest.") Briefly, we stopped outside the grotto's exit, at the rear.

"There. Your own little kingdom! Complete privacy! No one can ever eavesdrop or peek in. I mean, of course – not while the machinery's on! A curtain of brightness and shadow and sound will afford you full protection."

"Protection from what?" I asked.

"Well, what do you *think*, Semple? Protection from the parents!" He giggled. "Yes, even the most inquisitive and interfering of them! Even the most irritating and infuriating. Even the most demanding and unreasonable!"

He waited for me to giggle with him.

I did my best.

"Right, then," he said. "The moment has come. I feel we're ready to roll."

Roll? *Run*, more like it! As we walked into Santa's Grotto I was experiencing a major attack of the heebie-jeebies.

*

And so, very clearly, was the first of my customers...although I could see that he was doing his utmost to be brave.

"Hello, young man. And what's your name?" He'd been brought in by a tall and slim young woman dressed as Snow White.

"Andrew," he whispered. He was about six, a pretty little boy with fair hair and blue eyes. But he hung back mutely for a minute or so – until Snow White gave him a slight push, propelling him down the short and snowy slope towards my sleigh.

"Well, Andrew. Won't you climb in and sit beside me?"

He seemed increasingly uncertain. Suddenly his chin began to wobble. With a loud sob he buried his face in Snow White's

13

skirts – she had followed on, close behind. And he evidently didn't realize that the hand now patting his head was the selfsame hand which had sent him slithering down the slope. He must have supposed that he had slipped.

But as she firmly disengaged him I saw how sharp were her scarlet fingernails and how deeply she dug them in.

She heaved him up from behind, while I grasped him around the waist and pulled. He fell across my lap, like a newly landed fish.

"Ho-ho, my friend!" It wasn't easy but I manoeuvred him into the passenger seat as gently as I could. "Ho-ho, my merry little Andrew! But tell me now. Do you honestly *deserve* any nice things from Santa Claus this year?"

He'd caught his breath and ceased to sob. Petrified tears, however, still hovered fatly on his blond eyelashes.

"Well," I said, "I think perhaps you don't."

I looked at him. I was meant to add, "You see, the people you most love and trust have been spreading a lot of very nasty stories about you; and if we can't believe in those we trust, then who in the world *can* we believe in?"

But what I actually did say – pretty lamely and in a very hurried mumble – turned out to be something rather different.

"Well, I think perhaps you don't…have any need to worry! So now I'll strap you in and we can take our little trip."

Yet in spite of what I'd told him, and in spite of all my harried attempts to make him safe, he still shrank sobbingly from my side.

While as for me, only a moment later, it was just like somebody had seized my wrist and was jabbing at it with a needle. Relentlessly. At it and into it. Over and over. It was all that I could do to stop myself from screaming.

And well before the ride was ended, the boy was tugging at his safety strap. We hadn't even come to a standstill when he broke free of me and fled.

Mr Daglock whipped in.

He snapped at Snow White. "Oh, for pity's sake! Couldn't you have done something to prevent it? Have you absolutely *no* initiative?"

14

Then his glare returned to me. Without another word he yanked back my sleeve and stared at the shimmering, pale green bracelet.

From just my face, though, he must have seen the thing was working.

"Then what the blazes, Semple? Didn't His Lordship tell you what he wanted?"

I murmured that he had.

"Yes, I'm very sure he did! So what in heaven's name went wrong?"

I said I didn't know. I said I was sorry. Mercifully, the pain had now grown bearable – had diminished to a dull ache.

"*Sorry*, you clodhopper? *Sorry*? You think that's going to satisfy me? No – in future you'll just stick to your instructions; and stick to them, please, *as* if your very life depended on it! Your very *life*! Do you understand me, Semple? Are you capable of understanding?"

\*

Yes, I did. And, yes, I was. It seemed that they could overhear my every word. Watch my every move. I was completely powerless.

So from then on I had no choice whatever but to handle every child as though the time were Halloween.

But Halloween with a difference.

No treats.

All tricks.

# 6

I didn't sleep that night. Obviously – with my remaining in the toy department – I didn't have the weather to contend with; but there were worse things than weather to keep me awake.

You see, what haunted me was this. That period of transition in Park Lane: my offer to help out Lord Odin and his striding across the room to grip my hand – it had seemed as if he couldn't express his gratitude in any other manner! I remembered my gazing up at him from my extremely low armchair and noticing how much his eye had moistened. I remembered that my own vision had likewise grown misty – and that I'd thought how extra touching it was: the two of us bonding in this way.

But then? What then?

My left-hand sleeve... Either it had ridden back of its own accord or Lord Odin had displaced it. His fingers closed over the green plastic on my wrist – stayed there for several seconds, pressing down hard. Electricity pulsed through. The plastic gave a throb. But, no, *this* stuff couldn't be plastic, surely? It looked more like (oh, God, had I simply gone barmy?), it looked more like marble. More like a *bracelet* than just a hospital wristband. Even its colour had changed; had somehow acquired all the brightness of an emerald.

And then...well, yes, talk about barmy. Before one daft impression had properly taken hold, another had already elbowed it aside.

"Oh, look, Lord! Look! There on the balcony!"

"What?"

Lord Odin had been leaning over me; was for the moment facing away from the balcony.

"Out there, Lord! Out there on the railing! Look!"

Two black and gleaming birds were perching on the balustrade. Ravens! Although this time there wasn't any immediate departure, I instinctively knew – knew at the very instant their beady little eyes found mine – that these were the ravens I'd last seen by the river. And again I knew that they were evil.

16

Or, at any rate, emblems of evil.

But even before Lord Odin had moved more than a short way from me and had slowly turned about, I'd broken that chilling eyeball contact and struggled out of my chair – done so, indeed, with less effort than I should ever have thought possible. And was heading for the French windows.

I swiftly pulled one back and squeezed my way through.

Well, normally those birds would have frightened me. Yet today I could face them. Not only was I full of Dutch courage – I was often full of that! – but today I had Lord Odin's patronage, and his protection.

(Me and Lord Odin...thick as thieves and utterly invincible!)

"Your Lordship! These are the ravens that were spying on me earlier. And now they're spying on *you*. They don't mean either of us any good at all. Quite the opposite!"

It was disconcerting, though. Lord Odin stayed on the other side of the doorway. In fact, stood a fair distance back from it.

"Yes, highly interesting," he said. "Highly imaginative!"

Yet, for someone who had – only a minute ago – seemed pretty close to tears, his voice now sounded remarkably calm. Not in the least bit agitated.

"Come in, please. It's cold."

But first I had to scare them off. They were my enemies; this was my mission. I meant to show them that they couldn't intimidate *me*. Neither me nor my newfound friend. "Gotcha!" I would yell.

So I waved my arms at them.

Nothing happened.

My waving intensified.

Yet the ravens remained unflappable – continued merely to gaze at me: unblinking, baleful, glossy statuettes. I couldn't quite bring myself to give each of them a shove, but I decided I should thump the balustrade, set its wrought iron quivering, send tremors shooting up their claws, shock waves vibrating through their very gizzards.

But all at once I caught my foot on some blasted flowerpot or other. First I stumbled, then I sprawled. The breath was knocked out of me, and for a moment I thought I couldn't move – well,

17

not get up, anyway – perhaps I'd broken something? The stone beneath my palms felt wet, cold as a washed-down slab in a funeral parlour. Still the birds looked on – looked icily on – impervious to the biting wind. I waited for my friend to race out and assist me. Thank goodness for his energy and strength!

However, many seconds passed. Ten – fifteen – twenty? They went slowly; *very* slowly. "Your Lordship," I gasped. "Lord Odin! Lord!"

When at last, though, I managed to heave myself onto my knees, and then onto my feet, I saw that he was now sitting at his desk, maybe signing letters or writing cheques. He had his back towards me.

"Please close that door, Richard. Brrr! There's quite a draught in here. You had me wondering whether you were *ever* going to come in!"

Bewilderedly, I closed the door.

"But didn't you hear me calling?"

"Yes, yes. I saw the birds. They're often there. I assume they must live in the park."

"No, but I mean when..." Suddenly it all seemed so peculiar. "When I fell down just now."

"Oh, did you fall down? I'm so sorry. You should have cried out. You didn't hurt yourself, I trust?" He was smiling – but, disturbingly, I got the impression he was smiling more to himself than to me.

Then he rose from his desk and took my hands. He probably felt guilty and was doing what he could to compensate.

Yet, somehow, things had changed. They had most definitely changed; I was sure I wasn't simply imagining it. Somehow, his smile no longer seemed so pleasant.

He gave my cheek a playful pinch, as if acknowledging the cuteness of some toddler in a pushchair.

"Gotcha!" he said.

\*

"What!" I cried. (Gasped! *Yelped*!)

"Oh, yes! You lumbering slimeball! How could you ever have supposed otherwise? I've had my eye on you for some time."

But I couldn't believe what I was hearing. I absolutely could *not* believe what I was hearing!

"And you're priceless, Semple. D'you know that? Priceless. Not one good deed in half a lifetime; not one good deed, nor one kind word. Naturally," he went on, "I don't count anything you've said today – first buttering me up like a fruit scone, then spooning on the jam and clotted cream. Otherwise...nothing but surliness, self-pity and thinly veiled aggression. Yes, absolutely priceless! *Born* to be the figurehead on the bow of our prestigious new flagship, the *Hagalaz*: a brave and worthy galleon now bucking and straining at its anchor, waiting, *waiting*, until it can take on the world! Well, let's just say – for starters – until it can take on Oxford Street. Doesn't the thought of that excite you?"

Then he backed away and carefully wiped his fingers on his handkerchief.

"But oh my goodness! Don't you stink!"

His finger-wiping done, he clapped his hands.

"Longspoon! Come in here. Bring the others. I have decided! I have chosen! This useless old vagabond is *exactly* what we want. Ideal casting! And he's ours – all ours!"

He added, now standing by the hearth and dropping his handkerchief into the flames: "And he's very excited about it all! He's just told me."

Then for the next hour or so – or was it three or maybe four? – I received some very strange tuition.

But it occurred to me, resentfully, that if I was really worth spending so much time on, then in fact I couldn't be completely useless, could I? Old vagabond or not?

# 7

Eventually they let me go. But I remember nothing about leaving. About leaving the office, the building or even the street. I must have crossed several side roads. For all I know, cars may have had to skid to a standstill. Their drivers may have honked at me in fury, shaken their fists and hurled abuse through lowered windows. But I remember none of it.

A sudden realization, however – I don't know how it percolated through – finally jerked me out of my trance: the consciousness of loss, an absence of something comforting and familiar. There was nothing in my hands.

There was nothing in *either* of my hands. I became aware of this, and immediately went cold.

I hadn't got my carrier bags.

Dear God. I'd put them down beside the chair and promptly forgotten them.

Oh, no!

*No*!

Everything I owned, discounting what I wore, everything I owned was in those carrier bags. Not just bedding, that was the least of it, not just my spectacles, my toothbrush, my UB40, my knife and fork and spoon – none of those things mattered. But the manuscript I'd once written, a photograph, mementoes… All of these had gone, too.

And I couldn't do without them. It was as simple as that.

So I altered course. Instantly; instinctively. I altered course.

Didn't stop to think: am I returning into danger? Only thought: I want my carrier bags!

From Oxford Street to Marble Arch and back along Park Lane. Nos 8,9,10,11...

Outside No 12 there was someone else on duty. Older than the previous doorman. Shorter. Less pleasing to the eye.

But wait! Was that the only difference?

"Hey!" I cried. "This isn't No 12!"

"'Course it is. But move on now, there's a good feller, we don't want no beggars here."

I stared down at the man. I stared up at the building. Where were the spires, the turrets, the stained-glass windows?

The gargoyles? The balcony?

"Lord Odin's place? That's what I'm after."

"Who?"

"*Who*? Only the head of E.Y. Enterprises, that's who!"

"Never heard of him. Or it. Well, there's your answer, mate. So now shove off before there's any trouble."

Trouble? "I don't want any trouble. I've got the number wrong, that's all. I suppose it must be further down."

So, patently, not twelve. A hundred-and-twelve? Or two-hundred-and-twelve? Or twenty-one? Or – ?

Profusely sweating, panicking, befuddled, I blundered back and forth along Park Lane, back and forth, back and forth, on several occasions colliding with posh pedestrians who didn't get out of my way in time.

"Then who's this Lord Odin?" asked one doorman after another. They were all convinced I was imagining things. "E.Y. Enterprises? Ee, why, that's enterprising! Now you see us, now you don't! Completely staffed, no doubt, by little pink elephants?"

But I hadn't been imagining things. In one of my coat pockets I'd come across the letter addressed to Mr Scolopendrid at Hagalaz & Son which the double-crossing Lord Odin had written for me. ("You'll like him, Semple," he'd remarked. "Oh, he's delightful. Utterly delightful. They say he's extraordinarily like myself!") So, even if E.Y. Enterprises might dramatically have disappeared, this letter of introduction evidently hadn't.

Of course, I now knew only too well that I didn't want an introduction to any crony of Lord Odin. And especially not to any *clone* of Lord Odin. Yet somehow I appeared to have little say in the matter. It was as if a pair of remote-controlled hands had been placed in the middle of my back and was thrusting me forward with irresistible force.

In the direction of Marble Arch and Oxford Street again.

In the direction of Hagalaz & Son.

*

21

I've already said I got no sleep that night: simply going over and over things in my mind. But I suppose I must have got a little. A very little. Because, at about five the following morning, I was awoken by a scream.

# 8

And one scream was followed by another.

The first came when a woman thought she'd stumbled on a corpse.

The second (still hers) when the corpse opened its eyes and gazed at her in consternation.

"Strewth!" exclaimed the corpse. By this time it had managed, more or less, to pull itself up into a sitting position.

"Jeepers!" exclaimed the woman. By this time she had managed, more or less, not to fall down on top of it.

On top of *it*? No, I don't mean of *it*, for heaven's sake! I mean – of *me*!

Anyhow, I supposed that I owed her some word of explanation: in the prevailing gloom she could hardly have made out the red of the Santa trousers – even if my legs hadn't been partly covered by my overcoat, which I'd been using as a blanket. (Nor, I hoped, could she see the whisky bottle I now pushed closer to the counter. Last night, mysteriously, I'd found it behind one of the cushions on the sleigh: the single good thing to have emerged so far out of my experiences inside that wretched grotto.) So I gave a nod towards the belt and boots and pompommed hat, all lying on the counter. "Got taken on yesterday," I mumbled. "I mean – if it really happens to be any of your business!" I don't know why I added that. Even *I* felt that it hadn't been called for.

For a moment, though, she simply went on looking at me. She was pretty. About fifty, with auburn hair and a pleasant figure. Nice legs. She wore a scarf and overall. Rubber gloves. Fluffy mules – which were possibly pink.

"Here! But how about Muscle Mike?" she asked.

"What?"

"The overnight security man," she told me.

"Oh."

This was one of the reasons, of course, why I'd tucked myself behind the counter, carefully out of the path of any travelling torch beam. Admittedly, I'd forgotten the items of uniform which I'd left lying in full view.

Not that, so far as I was aware, any security man had in fact come up during the night. I hadn't heard any footsteps; and presumably *Muscle Mike* wouldn't have been wearing fluffy pink mules.

"Doesn't need to come up," she said. "Just has to sit there all cosy at his console and watch the monitors. Because they've got all them hidden cameras and stuff."

I didn't like the idea of that at all. Why, the man could be watching us right now! I glanced around guiltily. Made an effort to get up.

She reached out a hand. Then drew it back abruptly. Quickly turned away and seemed to gasp for air.

Of course, I felt a bit embarrassed. But mercifully, as if trying to conceal what she'd just done, she went on talking. Fast. "No, Muscle *Mick* is what I should've said. His sidekick, the real Muscle Mike, is only here by day – covers the main entrance. But if it's ever a choice between *him* and a starving cannibal...you choose the cannibal!"

I didn't bother mentioning that on the previous day, when it might have mattered, no starving cannibal had obligingly stepped forward.

Instead, I leant uncertainly against the counter. "Perhaps this one's got a softer nature?" I suggested.

"What – Muscle Mick? Yes, and perhaps *you're* the long-lost twin of Terry Wogan!" She studied me a moment. "So what were you doing at around eight o'clock last night, while the store was closing?"

"Hiding in the Gents." I gave a shrug. "I stayed there until everything seemed quiet."

But it hadn't been easy, I remembered: climbing up on the toilet seat, hoping to outwit the type of security guard who shone

23

his torch beneath the door of every cubicle. The gaps were nearly big enough to roll a Tonka through.

Though I didn't say any of this; I really wanted her to go. She was making it dangerous.

She asked: "So what about your staff pass?"

"Eh?"

"Haven't you been processed?"

I didn't know what she was on about.

"Still, love, if you haven't got one, then there's no need to worry, is there? Anyway, perhaps I shouldn't be standing here, jabbering away like this. Could be drawing attention to you."

"Yes, exactly!"

So then she began to move off, pulling her gimmicky little vacuum cleaner behind her – one of those cylindrical red and black ones, with a smiley face, and a flexible tube for a nose. She kicked up her feet as she went, like some poor man's Ginger Rogers. "Come on, Henry. I think we know when we're not wanted!" But she said it only lightly and it certainly didn't stop her turning back to me after a few seconds..

"Here! If you've been in this place all night, what have you had to eat?"

"Why?"

"Just curious, that's all!"

*Of course you are, madam*! But at least I didn't verbalize that. "Food doesn't interest me," I said.

"But what have you had?"

I informed her, in a rather bored tone, that up in the canteen yesterday I'd had a doughnut with my cup of tea.

"Oh well, then, nothing to worry about, is there? Plenty of nourishment in that. All food groups fully represented."

"Listen," I said. "I don't know who you are. But, to be honest, none of my eating habits need ever concern *you*."

And this time, I thought, it *was* justified. She deserved it. She may have had a nice face and she may have had kind intentions, yet all the same…enough was enough!

"Well, ever so sorry, I'm sure. Better leave you to get your sleep; seems like you need it! And tomorrow I'd better make a really big effort, hadn't I, just to tiptoe past, without so much as a single word?"

She gave Henry's hooter a jerk and they tootled off together, very haughtily.

But she threw back over her shoulder: "I mean, if you haven't already been chucked out by then! Which of course you will have! Or *my* name isn't Rita Whipplecrump!"

# 9

She proved to be mistaken, though.

A: I hadn't been chucked out by the following morning – plainly, Muscle Mick was less efficient than his colleague.

And B: she didn't have to make a big effort not to disturb me. Or, indeed, even a small one. Despite the fact that she arrived even earlier than before – maybe a whole hour earlier – I was already awake.

(It was funny. I appeared to get less rest with a proper roof over my head than when I'd just had the arch of some bridge to stretch out under, or that nice place at the rear of the Savoy Hotel. Perhaps, after so many years of sleeping rough, I simply needed my bag and a couple of bread pallets beneath me. Perhaps *anything else* would now have seemed unnatural!)

But, whatever the reason, I was ready for her when she came. Yes, blooming four a.m. or not. And when she did come I at least had the grace to offer her a mild apology.

She said: "Well, that's all right, then. And I'm sorry, too – for getting up on my high horse like I did. And as a peace offering," she added, "I was just about to leave you something."

Then she reached into her bucket where – amongst her cleaning utensils – there was a brown paper bag. She held it out to me.

"Here, what's this?"

"Your breakfast."

"Oh no," I said. "I can't be doing with charity!"

But even while I was making this protest, I remembered the sandwiches and plastic cups of tea or coffee – sometimes even soup – which, over the years, had been left beside me on the pavement. And, admittedly, I had never refused any of those, had I?

Yet, because they'd been anonymous, that had somehow made a difference.

"This is *not* charity!" She firmly shook her head.

"No, you're darned right it isn't. Because I can pay you for it!" I still had a couple of pounds remaining from my dole.

"Oh, don't be silly. It didn't cost me nothing."

"What, then?" I said,sarcastically. "You mean, you stole it?"

"Yes, very funny. But what I do mean is: I work in a snack bar, and what you got there is leftovers."

"Leftovers?" In the bag lay two ham rolls and a wedge of apple pie. Each was wrapped in clingfilm. And I now gave one of the rolls an energetic squeeze. "This doesn't feel like leftovers to me," I muttered.

"Well, you'll just have to excuse it, then, won't you? But whether you like it or not, they *are* leftovers – yesterday's – and rather than throw them in the bin, I happened to think of *you*. Didn't know it was against the law."

"Hmm," I said, slowly returning the money to my pocket. "Well all right, then. In that case…"

"And I've brought you some coffee, as well. You'd better have another good grumble." From the larder in her cleaning bucket she defiantly produced a small flask.

I fixed my attention on the paper bag. Even in this poor light, even without my specs, I could read the name of the snack bar. Millie's. In Paddington Street. I knew it well. I had never been in, but had passed it often enough. "What – you work there, then? A day job…*as* well *as* working in this place?"

"Yes. Though I'm only there part-time, more's the pity! Otherwise I'd be out of here quicker than you could say Rita Whipplecrump!"

"My word! You can't mean, then, you're not *happy* to be at Hagalaz & Son, so bright and early every morning?"

It was a joke; she acknowledged as much with a weak smile. "I wouldn't be happy at Hagalaz & Son at *any* time." She shook her head and pursed her lips. "But no other time could be half as awful as *this*," she remarked.

"It couldn't?"

"No. And I'm not even talking about the rotten pay, or the boredom, or the lack of decent colleagues – three silly teenagers who just giggle amongst themselves whenever I try to be friendly! No, I'll tell you straight, Mr Semple. It's something else that gets to me."

"What, then?"

She answered with unexpected simplicity.

"The spookiness of the place."

"Eh?"

"Don't tell me *you* don't feel it the same as I do?"

The light was just so dim at night, she said; the central gangway so long and straight and empty. You were always looking over your shoulder, always imagining you might have seen some movement or heard some noise, always straining to make out what you hoped was only a mannequin – or a grouping of mannequins – repositioned on the previous day. She made it sound like a ghost story.

I'd never read a ghost story set in a department store but I could certainly see what she meant: all that draughty space and all those unfamiliar shapes looming through the shadows. All those pillars and paths and intersections.

All that silence. And all those elusive creaks and sighs and rustlings. Even I, having had a little too much to drink the night before, had thought it was a bit like bedding down inside Madame Tussaud's – what's more, inside the very Chamber of Horrors: amongst the toys there was actually a model of the Grim Reaper, complete with scythe! My God! No wonder that she shivered.

"Yes, there's something about the atmosphere," she said. "It's not..."

She chose her words with care.

"Healthy. Or normal. Or...*good*."

27

Just at that moment, my wrist was gripped by the same agonizing pain I'd had three weeks ago – and, once again, I nearly cried out.

But I swore, instead.

"Not healthy! Not *good*! We are, I suppose, still talking about a department store in the middle of Oxford Street? At the start of the twenty-first century?"

She offered no response.

"Oh, what rubbish!" I exclaimed.

We stared at one another; I tried not to let her see the pain I was in. I don't know why. Wouldn't it have been better if she had?

"In any case, " I added, "there's nobody *forcing* you to work here, is there?"

I thought I saw the glint of tears; felt sure my unfriendliness would finally see her off. (Well, good riddance! Just leave me to deal with this dreadful pain in private!)

"If you must know," she said, "my husband isn't well. His days go very slow. In the evenings he likes to have me there with him."

I supposed she meant this only left the early mornings to fit in a second job. She was at Millie's from eleven till four.

"So your old man's out of work? Bit of a layabout, is he?"

"No, he is *not!* Never had a day off sick, until…" She shrugged. "Oh, life isn't fair," she said, "and never was, and never will be – "

She stopped.

"Here – I'm sorry! I got provoked. I don't have to tell *you* about life not being fair. You, of all people."

The pain was easing. I wanted to apologize. (Being myself, of course, a bit of a layabout.) "Oh, well. Me? I muddle through. I mean, no good whingeing about things, is it?"

"Saying, in other words, that's what you think I'm doing?"

"Eh? No! Nothing of the sort!"

But she still seemed doubtful. "Well, all right, then. You enjoy your breakfast. I suppose I'd better get on with my job – without whingeing about it, if I can. I'll come back later for the flask."

On her return, though, she didn't seem to care whether I'd enjoyed the ham rolls and fruit pie and coffee, even though I told her twice how good they had all been. She was clearly in a sulk. All she wanted to know was: didn't I think the time had come for taking cover in the Gents? Before Mr Daglock and his little band of lackeys turned up, like a squad of field mice, she said, with noses and whiskers all a-twitch, to sniff out any sticky fingerprints she might have missed, or sweet wrappers, or bits of chewing gum, or *anything* in fact that had no right to be there. She stared at me, ironically.

I'd been planning to ask her to get me – with the two pounds I still had left – a toothbrush, some toothpaste and a flannel.

But, plainly, this wasn't a good moment.

# 10

Yet, after this, things improved – at least, where my work wasn't concerned, they did. Every morning for the next three weeks Mrs Whipplecrump brought me coffee and leftovers…leftovers, so-called. I couldn't reimburse her – not that she would have allowed me to – because, puzzlingly, I hadn't yet received any wages. Nothing apart from my luncheon vouchers and the bottle of whisky that turned up at the back of the sleigh each evening. So it would have been silly and pointless, wouldn't it, to get all stroppy again over my sensitivity regarding charity?

That didn't stop me, though, from getting all stroppy over other things.

Even on Christmas Eve – when I naturally supposed this was the last time I'd be seeing her.

"Somebody left a newspaper in the Gents," I said; possibly sounding even more surly than usual. "And what do you think I saw in it? Only this very stupid photograph, with a few lines of very stupid description underneath."

"Mmm?"

"About some idiot Father Christmases...three of them...at stores in Nottingham and Manchester and Aberdeen? Or it might have been Aberystwyth – *I* don't know!"

"What about them?" She gave a laugh. "Or do you mean it came as a shock, to discover *you* weren't the only one?"

"The only what?"

"The only real Santa! Or perhaps you didn't realize there's a load of cheeky impostors out there, all pretending to be you? Honestly, the nerve!"

I guessed she was only trying to tease me out of my sullen frame of mind but shouldn't she have known this wasn't what was needed? I thought women were supposed to be intuitive.

"Oh, for heaven's sake! Please don't try to be clever – I'm not in the mood! People have been complaining about them, that's all. It seems odd. I can't see what's going on. Or where it can be leading."

"Where what can be leading?"

"Why, what I'm *telling* you about! Or aren't you listening?"

"Yes, I'm listening. Can't say I'm understanding."

"Oh, never mind. Sorry I brought it up. Had some foolish idea it might have been important. You must try to forgive me!"

Stroppy? Me? Good gracious, how could anyone think that?

She sighed.

"Well, speaking for myself, Mr Semple, I don't know nothing of any complaints about *any* Father Christmases, if that's what's troubling you. Perhaps it's nothing new; perhaps people have always complained about Father Christmases. For instance – only last night over supper – my Fred was saying he couldn't think where they manage to dredge up all these really odd characters each year to..."

But then she broke off and was plainly flustered.

"Oh, yes, Mrs Whipplecrump?" I myself remained deceptively calm. "What was it that your Fred was saying? All these really odd characters they manage to dredge up each year to...to do *what*, precisely?"

"And no one's made any sort of complaint against *you*, have they? Seems to me that's all you need to worry about."

"But you forgot to finish your sentence," I persisted, reasonably. "What was it your Fred was saying...only last night, I mean, over supper?"

At this point, however, she became defiant. "I'll tell you *one* thing my Fred was saying! And saying several times over, too! Today is Christmas Eve – right? And on top of doing all my usual hours, I've been ordered to return here at eight this evening! Eight till twelve. To tidy up before the holidays! Special orders of the management! So what's his game, then, old Mr Skinflint Scolopendrid? And who can tell me what's so very different about *this* year – and why it's got to be just *this* floor? Well, anyway, you should've listened to my Fred going on about it! Working till midnight! Christmas Eve! Without so much as a single please or thank-you – and certainly not signed *Yours lovingly, Old Meanypants*, with kisses underneath and a *PS: Hope you'll enjoy your Christmas box!"*

Mrs Whipplecrump laughed, despite her indignation. But her laughter didn't last. "And I ask you, Mr Semple, what will the buses be like after midnight? Will there even be any? Perhaps I ought to send *him* a little love note, too, requesting he lay on a limousine for me. D'you think he might agree to it?"

She gave another short laugh.

"Or lay *under* a limousine for me? It being Christmas and all? Season of giving and goodwill."

I nodded my approval, even though in fact I'd never once set eyes upon the wretched man.

Her tone changed.

"*You'll* still be here, though, won't you? At around eight?" She seemed to ask it with some urgency.

"Well, who knows?" I said.

"But I'm counting on you being here! Not that I can really imagine people bringing their kids to see Father Christmas as late as seven or eight on Christmas Eve. Pack them off to bed early, that was always *my* motto. Still, knowing this lot, they won't let anybody leave ahead of time. Not even Santa Claus. But at least that means I shan't be turning up to a completely empty building: just me here and Muscle Mick in the control room. Oh, heavens, Mr Semple. Sounds like a real recipe for fun, *that* does!"

# 11

Night came. I might be out of a job now, but I'd not been richer in years: Mr Daglock had just presented me with five hundred pounds...in cash! (Our first-day disagreements presumably forgotten?) Five hundred smackeroos! There'd also been a bottle of Scotch – at no point mentioned by anyone – lying in concealment in the usual place. I shuffled off to the Gents with all this precious booty. I'd decided to spend another night sleeping in the department and simply to wait and see what the following day would bring.

But, of course, my thinking had been faulty. On my careful return from the toilets, I saw Mrs Whipplecrump standing by the counter at which she always found me in the mornings. She looked anxious.

"Oh, Mr Semple! I thought you'd gone!"

"No, my dear."

I exclaimed over the great plateful of supper she'd put down on the counter. Tonight I hadn't expected so much as a cheese sandwich.

Then I told her of my plan.

But she only shook her head.

"Oh, no, it wouldn't work," she said. "I'm afraid you'll have to leave the store when I do – otherwise you're going to be a prisoner here till after Boxing Day. And you'd starve, Mr Semple. Don't you realize that? Over Christmas you would starve."

"Why?" I gave a nod towards the meal she'd brought me. "*This*'ll keep me going for some time! And then there's always the Food Hall on the ground floor; and, besides that, not a soul to interfere with me over the whole of the holidays..."

Because, I thought, if our friend the security guard – security guard Mark 2 – hadn't so far bothered with me, why on earth should he begin to do so now, when I was practically all set to make my fond farewells and bow out of Hagalaz forever?

And, my goodness, I would even be able to kip down on one of those fancy orthopaedic beds in the Furniture Department. I could tell myself I was residing at the Dorchester.

But in the meanwhile I promised Mrs Whipplecrump that I should naturally proceed with caution.

"No, there'd still be somebody around," she answered, a bit vaguely. "And then you'd only end up in a police cell and I don't suppose you'd really care for that."

Think so? Try me. Sounds restful. Perhaps not quite up to the Dorchester but even so...

However, in a mild attempt to be obliging, I agreed that I'd do everything I could to avoid spending Christmas in jug.

"But what *are* you going to do?" This might have been the sixth or seventh time she'd asked.

And the sixth or seventh time that I'd pretended not to hear.

"Well, then, listen to me!" (She said this with a sudden fierce air of there's-going-to-be-no-argument-about-this.) "You'll be coming to ours to eat your Christmas dinner!"

"No. That's very kind of you. But no."

"Give me one reason why not."

Well, it seemed that I'd been learning. I didn't say, as I definitely would have only three weeks earlier, *No, I'm not after handouts*! *If you want to play Lady Bountiful please go to play her somewhere else*!

Now all I replied was:

"I just think your husband wouldn't be too chuffed!"

"Oh – ," she began.

"Nor your daughter. And didn't you say that she was bringing her fiancé?"

"Well, so what if she is? I've had a word with Fred. And I've also had a word with Tina..." But I could see this wasn't true. "And we're all agreed on it – that Christmas isn't any time for being on your own."

"But I shan't be on my own. I shall be amongst my pals and that's exactly how it should be: celebrating with whichever of 'em may be looking for a spot of company. Because – all right, I do admit it – loneliness *can* sneak up on you over Christmas."

Whilst saying this, I shambled over to a nearby chair: one of the few put out for customers. And, although I certainly offered it to Mrs Whipplecrump, I felt pleased when she refused. My legs felt tired.

"Yet it isn't so bad as you might think," I then continued. "Usually, you see, we get our lunch at a Crisis shelter. It's good food and the atmosphere's matey. And after that – well, last year, anyway – a few of us strolled up to St Paul's and drank a toast to Baby Jesus...who, if you think about it, also went on to be an outcast without any fixed abode."

"Yet even so," she remarked, "it don't seem right. You're a stubborn man, Mr Semple."

But she clearly didn't know what else she could do about it, so after a further moment she gave another of her elaborate sighs – then, with her duster at the ready, moved over to the life-sized model of a reindeer which stood three or four feet away, beside the central aisle. She had once told me this model was one of the few things she really liked in the department.

"Heigh ho! Better get on, I suppose, if there's nothing I can say to make you change your mind. Better get on and leave you to enjoy your supper."

My supper. There was turkey and stuffing, roast potatoes, sprouts and gravy, all visible beneath a wrap of clingfilm. Now, as I got up from my chair and lifted the plate off the counter...

"Sweet Fanny Adams," I cried, "this is *hot*!"

She knew I didn't mean I'd burnt myself, only that I didn't see how anything could have come out of the oven at her place, travelled here on the bus, and *still* be holding so much heat.

"I microwaved it!" she exclaimed, more cheerfully. "Microwaved it down in Kitchen Appliances. Took a chance that you-know-who wouldn't see me."

I'd forgotten all about microwaves.

She added as an afterthought: "Your still being here, though, makes me wonder if he ever sees *anything* – outside the pages of his Beano or his Dandy!"

34

I sat down and rested my meal on my lap. I said somewhat gruffly: "I've appreciated all this."

"Well, it's been nice having you around," she said. "Next week I'm going to miss you. The really sad bit is..."

There was a silence.

I asked her what the really sad bit was.

But still she hesitated.

"Oh, I don't know. Eh, Blitzen? Well, if only we had a bigger house for starters. Or if only my old man could somehow see it all a bit different. Or if only we had a neighbour with a granny flat to let..."

I interrupted, sharply. "Why do you call him Blitzen?"

"Oh, Blitz!" She seemed almost relieved. "Do you hear what that funny man is saying? Because I just *know* that's who you are, don't I, my poppet?"

She gave his nose a quick polish. Then, with her arms around his neck, she nuzzled her cheek against his mane – all of which struck me as being not only contrived but excessively sentimental. False gaiety should be saved strictly for pantomimes.

However, even worse was to come. She actually began to sing.

> "Blitzen the red-nosed reindeer
> Had a very shiny nose,
> And if you ever saw it
> You might even say…
> It glows!"

She performed a little dance, as well. A dance, moreover, which she concluded with a curtsey!

"You know, I used to be in the church choir, Mr Semple." (I refrained from asking whether it was the singing or the dancing they had wanted her for.) "Haven't quite lost it yet, have I?"

I also refrained from asking, "Lost what? The plot?"

She reminisced. "You know, when I was a child I dreamt of becoming a star in one of them big musicals. Sometimes *really* dreamt about it, I mean."

35

Oh dear. What a shame! A plateful of delicious food which she'd plainly hoped was going to be a treat...and now my stomach was being twisted into knots and I was getting the kind of indigestion which might hang around for days.

"Oh, but why did you have to choose *that* song?" I cried out, angrily. "*That* song out of all the others?"

"Why? What's the matter with it?"

"I can't stand it, that's what's the matter with it! Do I need to furnish reasons? With all my i's crossed and my t's dotted?"

If I hadn't made that ridiculous mistake it might have ended up as before, with her prancing off in a huff.

But, instead, she only laughed.

"Oh, you just get some of that nice warm food inside you, while I go and disinf...while I go and clean out that great big fancy grotto of yours. Urgent instructions from Mr Maurice Meanypants himself! Won't take me long, though..." She waved her duster around. "Swish, swish, swish! See…the job's half done already! Really, Old Skinflint doesn't *deserve* us, does he, Mr Semple?"

"No, Mrs Whipplecrump," I said – by now starting to feel better and only wanting, yet again, to atone. "He most definitely doesn't."

Then she went away, quite chirpily, and for once, it seemed, not giving a moment's thought to anything that might be lurking in the shadows: aliens, ghosts, werewolves, murderers, you name it: unauthorized presences of more or less any description.

Which – in the light of what was to come – could be seen as being just a fraction ironic.

To say the very least.

# 12

Because... There was a young man leaning against one of the pillars.

Maybe not actually lurking.

Maybe not at a spot where the shadows had clustered at their deepest and darkest.

But someone who was certainly an unauthorized presence.

He stood with his arms folded, his legs crossed at the ankles. For a person who had no business to be there, his attitude seemed remarkably relaxed.

Far more so than mine. When I caught sight of him I jumped and nearly sent the plateful of food skimming off my lap.

And that was before he had even spoken.

"I don't know, Richard, whether Old Skinflint deserves you or not." Despite the easiness of his demeanour he sounded stern – almost angry. "And, frankly, I don't care. To me the question is: do you deserve Old Skinflint?"

\*

So here – at last – was that dreaded security guard. By no means unauthorized.

But all he'd had to do was to stay away a few more hours! Or, at the very most, a few more days...that is, if I'd ignored Rita Whipplecrump's advice.

Blast him, I thought.

Yes, blast him – infuriating man – irredeemably perverse!

\*

Yet *no*!

On second thoughts, I must have got the whole thing wrong. Of course he was unauthorized. He had to be.

Had to be.

Because a security guard would be in uniform, wouldn't he? This man was wearing faded blue jeans, white trainers, white T-shirt. Admittedly the jeans looked laundered, the trainers unscuffed, the T-shirt nicely pressed. But I had the notion that cleanliness would never be a substitute for formality in the eyes of the management of Hagalaz & Son.

Besides. The fellow was far too lightly dressed for night-time in a department store in the middle of winter. At night-time there wasn't any central heating.

And talking of the management...I felt a security guard would never speak of Mr Scolo-Whatsit with anything but respect. A security guard (unless, of course, he were off-duty...in the pub, say, complaining to his mates of being overworked and underpaid) would never refer to his employer as Old Skinflint – surely he wouldn't? It could so easily get to the wrong ears. It could so easily mean the sack.

Also, on that very first morning, Rita Whipplecrump had scoffed at my suggestion that Muscle Mick might have a nicer nature than she gave him credit for. So from then on I'd pictured him almost as a doppelgänger of his workmate: a doppelgänger of that mean-featured, bull-necked lump of lard I'd met on my arrival. The missing link.

But this man here – despite the impression he gave of severity or anger – didn't come across as a natural inhabitant of the gutter. Nor even of the dark. (Well, semi-dark.) In fact, it now struck me how clearly I could see him. By some trick of the light, the habitual night-time gloom had all but withdrawn from around the pillar where he stood.

Or, rather, against which he lolled.

I'd never noticed such a trick of the light before.

So who was he? It was a mystery. As I say, he certainly didn't seem shifty.

No. *He* certainly didn't seem shifty.

"You're probably surprised to find me here?" I stammered.

He shook his head.

"But I was just on my way out, you see. I've had to stop a bit late because..." I looked at my plate, put down the knife and fork I'd been holding. I gave him a weak, conciliatory smile – though, possibly, I gave it more to the floor than to him.

"Richard," he returned, quite gently. "There's simply no point to this if you are going to lie!"

No point to what? And, come to think of it, this was the second time he'd called me Richard. Previously, I must have been so startled it hadn't fully registered.

"How do you know my name?"

He didn't answer.

"Oh, yes, of course! You've been eavesdropping."

He shrugged. "I know more than just your name."

"But nothing you won't have overheard!"

Then I realized that Mrs Whipplecrump had never called me Richard. She only used my surname.

"Nothing I won't have overheard? Well, let me see, now. Did you ever mention *this*, for instance? How on the afternoon you got here you thought briefly about killing yourself?"

"What!"

"Yes. You were standing on the edge of the pavement and some buses went by. Or had you forgotten?"

No, I had not forgotten.

"And did you happen to mention that – occasionally – you were still thinking of it?"

"You know damned well I didn't." My voice was practically a croak. "Just who...? Who in the world *are* you?"

"Somebody who takes an interest."

"Oh, yes. An interest...? In what – giving people the fright of their lives? Confusing them?"

His mood seemed to lighten a little. "No. Not people in general. Yourself in particular. Mainly an interest in you and an interest in Christmas."

I had no idea how to answer. I suppose I could simply have asked, "Why?" But, instead: "Huh! You make it sound as though there's some connection."

"Do I? How extraordinary! Oh – and by the way – your costume's a complete disgrace. But you're already aware of that, aren't you?"

I was still in fact wearing the costume...all but the hat, which I'd thrown off on leaving the grotto. But I hadn't thought of it as stealing, my not removing the jacket and trousers – those very badly torn jacket and trousers! – nor could I believe he had come after me merely to retrieve them.

(The boots might have been a different matter. I could well understand the management's wanting to retrieve *those*.)

"You think I'm wanting to step into your boots?" the young man inquired.

Obviously, this followed on from absolutely nothing...but it was still a huge coincidence!

"Hey, I'm sorry," he exclaimed. "I forgot. The name is Bill."

He walked towards me now and held out his hand on reaching me.

But I didn't offer him my own. I, too, gave an exclamation.

"Oh, what a fool I am! I should have realized. Lord Odin sent you here! It was him who wanted you to snoop."

"Sent here by Odin? *Lord* Odin, to boot. Oh, Richard, what an insult!"

Yet, unexpectedly, he laughed.

"So that's why you wouldn't shake hands? Well, I'm relieved. But – gracious, no – I haven't been sent by Odin."

"Then by who? The fairies at the bottom of your garden?"

"No." He slowly shook his head again – though with a further friendly grin, to pay passing tribute to this priceless example of wit. "No," he repeated...and then paused. "I was sent here neither by Odin nor by the fairies at the bottom of my garden. I was sent here on the very special orders of..."

He broke off and looked at me provocatively.

"The suspense is killing me," I said.

"I thought it might be. On the very special orders," he finished, "of the President of STARS."

# 13

Now that was what did it! I let out a great guffaw. It wasn't even phoney. For – suddenly – I had understood.

Yes. It so happened that a little earlier I'd taken just a nip or two of Scotch. And I could remember thinking as I'd done so, "Well, thank my lucky stars – at least I've still got *this* to bring me comfort!"

Stars! You see? Stars! I'd got them on the brain. This fellow was a figment of my imagination. Like little pink elephants. Or like a six-foot-tall, invisible white rabbit...ever hear of *Harvey*? Or like some bright-eyed young clever clogs who could do nothing but speak to you in riddles.

"Ah, indeed! The President of Stars," I said, pretending to have difficulty in becoming suitably straight-faced again. "And who's he when he's at home?"

Yet that was purely me wanting to show how light-heartedly I was taking it. Because – obviously – the only thing I had to do to get rid of him was to snap my fingers and ignore him. I knew that now.

This knowledge was exhilarating.

Except that...

Well, I'd have thought anyone, absolutely anyone, could snap his fingers. I suppose I'd somehow never tried.

All right. Failure acknowledged. But at least I could carry out the rest of it. Completely ignore him.

Although – after a full half-minute of gazing up at various corners of the ceiling, humming a pop tune and unthinkingly tapping my foot to its infectious rhythm – well, damn it, when I slowly looked down again, he was still there.

"Oh, skedaddle!" I said; forgetting Abba and employing the tactics of an Old Testament authority figure instead – naturally, a prophet rather than a dancing queen was going to be required. I tried to look granite-faced and undeniable. I said, "That is the way. Walk ye in it!" I think I was quoting correctly. I think it was Jeremiah I was quoting.

41

But nothing was achieved. My sternly pointing finger might have gone on sternly pointing for all time.

Well, then. It clearly needed great reserves of cunning to outsmart this bright Sir Galahad who could have come straight off the set of a Persil ad – great reserves to point out, very patiently, how he must have been fed unreliable information and regrettably sent to the wrong address. How therefore he should simply cut his losses and go home.

In short, I decided on an entirely new approach.

"Why, it's a good job, young fellow, that I'm not a drinking man, ha, ha! For if I *had* been – ha, ha! – I might have thought it quite normal to hallucinate. But since I've now been on the wagon for years and years it must be very plain, mustn't it, that you've merely mistaken your destination? I *am* sorry. Life's such a bummer!" And I flicked my hands at him; maybe in the manner of some monarch terminating an audience he wished he'd never granted. "Goodbye," I said. "Safe journey back!"

Now *there* was cunning for you. *There* was diplomacy.

However. The hallucination only smiled at me. He was plainly of the obstinate variety. Annoyingly thick-skinned.

"I must show you how to do that," he offered.

"Oh, for heaven's sake! Do what?"

And would you believe it? The impertinent pup! He snapped his fingers! He snapped his fingers once – twice – three times. He should have known, of course: no way would I put up with that!

"Like whistling," he said. "Easy once you've got the knack."

"Oh, go *a-way*!" I snarled.

"Ah, sorry. I forgot. You can't whistle either, can you?"

He took a yo-yo off a shelf and casually began to play with it.

"And you've abstained from alcohol since...since *when*, did you say? *How* many years, did you say?"

I couldn't think what to do. As a first step, I leaned down and put my supper on the floor. It felt stupid to be sitting there holding onto a dinner plate; let alone being given a yo-yo display by a pesky apparition.

"Because you see, Richard, you're not fooling anyone. Fooling them, for instance, about that whisky bottle hidden under there."

And he indicated the counter.

Having done so, he began to wander around a bit. Oddly enough, I noticed that he, too, stopped to stroke the reindeer – just like Mrs Whipplecrump before him – not just to stroke it but even to speak to it. And he appeared to be talking to the other animals, as well. Not just the animals. You might have thought that right here in the department he had dozens of good friends all anxious to be warmly greeted!

While he was engrossed in this way I stumbled to my feet and sidled over to the counter, fully to reassure myself about my alcohol being safe. It was, of course. I had hidden it beneath an old placard.

But all the same I felt rattled – because I knew I'd been alone when I'd concealed it. You soon become aware if anyone is watching you. I mean, if he's there in the room with you, as this bloke must have been – not sitting at some far-off console.

"I don't see where you get your information from," I grumbled, after he'd returned from his meanderings through Wonderland.

He shrugged. "From TV, mostly."

"Oh, naturally! Of *course*! Reality programmes? Nature programmes? *Big Brother*?"

"Well, yes – in a way. But it's a TV so advanced it goes straight to the heart of things." He paused. "Literally. It explores and documents the workings of a person's heart."

*Then how about the workings of a madman's heart?* I had nearly asked this but had suddenly thought it might be safer not to. I'd begun to wonder if he could be dangerous.

You see, I have to be honest here. Almost from the outset I'd been struggling to convince myself that he *was* a hallucination. Because...well, if he wasn't...then it all became a lot more scary. Obviously! Scary and sinister *and* dangerous.

"Richard, the only danger at the moment – for you – is that you won't come clean with me. The only danger at the moment – for us – is that you may persist in thinking I'm a lunatic."

Oh, strewth!

"Oh, strewth," I said, "I really do need a pull of this!"

And I reached down for my whisky.

But hardly had I started to unscrew it than the bottle was whipped out of my hand. Though not by him. Nor by anyone, apparently. I was already stunned but what I saw now left me speechless. Or what I *thought* I saw now.

I thought I saw the bottle float towards the ceiling.

What?!!!

But nobody or nothing was going to make off with *my* bottle! Oh, no! Steal it from beneath my very nose! I was galvanized by utter fury, by sheer moral indignation! I had once been a trophy-winning athlete: college king of track and field. I became that man again. You should have seen me almost leap onto that counter!

Yet now it wasn't any silver cup that I was after.

But sadly – although my repeated efforts to yank back the bottle *were* so galvanized – the slippery glass eluded me each time. Kept hovering fractionally beyond my straining reach.

And at last I could do nothing but stand there open-mouthed on the counter.

Totally gutted.

My fury, however, had now changed back to something far closer to fear. Not that I'd exactly lost my bloody-mindedness.

Nor my curiosity.

"How did you *do* that?"

"Ah," he replied. "Tricks of the trade!"

"Magic?" I thought I heard a quaver in my tone.

"Magic? You always say you don't believe in anything like that. I mean, in anything that has no rational explanation."

Fear or no fear, quaver or no quaver, I at once grew angry again. "How do *you* know what I always say?"

I got down from the counter. (Damn it, he had to help me; although at least he did so without appearing to notice.) But, back on the floor, I couldn't stop my eyes from returning to the ceiling – even as I answered my own question.

"Oh, yes. Naturally! Human Heart TV!"

"Dick, old chap, I really think you're learning."

"It was meant to be sarcastic."

"I realize that. But even so..."

"Can't I *please* have my bottle back?"

The young man smiled but gently shook his head. "As a matter of fact you said it in The White Swan – oh, just about six weeks ago. About not believing in anything that can't be proven."

The White Swan... Yes, I remembered going into The White Swan – remarkably – because it was the only time I'd ever been there. I'd gone with a couple of pals and the landlord hadn't been too keen to serve us. Especially not before he'd seen the colour of our money.

"And you, I take it, were crouching down behind the bar?" More sarcasm...as I hoped he would appreciate.

"No. I wasn't near the place. Not even disguised as a fruit machine, nor as the cat curled up on the windowsill. Remember noticing that cat?"

"Huh! Who ever notices a cat?"

"That's funny: I could have sworn he made you think of Bombles. For the first time in ages you suddenly caught yourself thinking fondly of old Bombles."

And that was finally what did it: in conjunction with the bottle and all the rest of it: this reference to a long-dead ginger tom. It toppled my defences.

# <u>14</u>

There was so much giggling coming from the children's bedroom that I thought I had better investigate. But they had a crayoned notice pinned to the door: "Please don't come in without nocking." Clearly, though, there'd been some second thoughts attached to this. "Please don't come in even if you do nock. Dangerous animal. First day in zoo." (*More* second thoughts.) "Or maybe circus. Be warned. Keep out." I stood and listened. The dangerous animal was obviously providing a lot of jollity.

45

Peter was eight, Naomi a year younger. Peter wasn't our original choice of name; we'd been going to call him Simon but had then realized that at school he'd almost certainly be known as Semple Simon. Nevertheless, we'd still wanted to name him for the same disciple.

I knocked on the door. There came a startled silence.

"How's the dangerous animal?"

"Go away, Dad. He's a surprise. You'll see him later."

"Not him! Her!" called out Naomi; and immediately there was a fresh cascade of giggles. "We'd like to let you in, Daddy, but we're still training him – I mean, her."

"Besides, you'll have to buy a ticket to come in, and my stupid assistant hasn't printed them yet."

"Stupid yourself!" replied his assistant, who could always be relied upon to give every bit as good as she got. "I'm busy at the moment stopping this dangerous animal from wanting to eat people; from wanting to gobble them all up, every last chunk of flesh and every last drop of blood. Eyes and nose and ears and everything."

"Goodness," I said. "How are you managing that?"

"I'm giving him Smarties."

"That's resourceful," I said. "Thank heaven. But what happens when he's eaten up all the Smarties?"

"You'll have to run and buy us some more, please, Daddy? Only, don't forget that it's a she, not a he. And she has this little song...except we'll most prob'ly need to sing it for her."

"Hey, stop it, you silly! Why've you got to be giving away *all* our secrets? Dad? What time will Mum be getting back?"

"In about an hour."

"Can't wait to see what she's bought," said Naomi – in the midst, presumably, of struggling to satisfy a roaring and insatiable appetite. "And I can't wait, either, to see what the something special is which you're cooking us for tea."

At that time we were living near Dover, and Harriet had gone into Canterbury to buy herself an evening dress; if she couldn't find the right one she'd have to continue the search the following Saturday. It had to be absolutely the right one, because – in eleven days from now – we'd be shaking hands with the Queen and Prince Philip, not to mention seeing again some of my wartime buddies; being introduced to their wives; and maybe meeting a number of elder statesmen and show business personalities, as well. This was to be at a Royal Command Performance in Leicester Square. Ten years earlier I had flown one of the planes in a bombing raid which the film commemorated.

I said: "Okay, I'll leave you to it. Have fun. But by the way – how do you spell knocking?"

"That's a lucky coincidence," replied my cheeky firstborn. "It's written on the door. You can get it from there."

More giggles, of course.

I told them how to spell knocking.

"Very good, Daddy," said Naomi. "You can now go to the top of the class."

"Dad, it doesn't matter where you go, so long as you're a nice man and just *go*."

In fact, I went to fetch them a reinforcement of Smarties. I was warmly thanked...and told to leave it on the landing.

When Harriet came home we were both allowed in – perhaps partly on account of the Smarties, partly on account of Naomi's impatience to nip into our bedroom and peek at the new dress, perhaps partly because all that grooming and training were beginning to grow wearisome – we were both allowed in to see the wild animal, without even being asked to pay admission. (*Still* no tickets printed. In fact, though, we promised a couple of shillings to cover admission for the pair of us.) Bombles – or rather, for this occasion, Bombelina – was taking time off from eating people and was stretched out on his (her?) back, with all four paws sticking in the air and a soporific, supremely soppy expression, patently imploring that the tickling shouldn't stop.

In order to meet his public, he had been winsomely decked out. From the dressing-up box had come an old pink nightie of Harriet's, considerably cut down, although pink and ginger didn't *always* go; from their own chest of drawers, a yellow ribbon to tie round his waist, two pairs of white ankle socks – with elastic bands to hold them up – and Peter's green woolly hat with two chestnut-coloured bobbles...I wondered if his

47

grandmother, who did *not* enjoy knitting, would have felt intensely gratified by this.

But all in all it was a pretty sharp outfit. Harriet exclaimed and went down on her knees and took her stipulated turn at tummy-rubbing. "Sweet Bombelina – oh, yes, sorry, darling, most *savage* Bombelina" (this, addressed to Naomi) – "are you truly going to sing for us?"

And, indeed, if the volume and resonance of his purr were anything to go by, he could possibly have topped the bill at the Palladium.

"Yes, but he's shy, Mummy. Wants us to do it for him. Besides, it's *about* him; says it might seem a bit like showing off. And anyway! We're the ones who made it up."

"What do you mean: *we* are?"

"I helped, didn't I? I wrote just as much of it as you did! Prob'ly more, if you really want to know."

However – after a good deal of giggling and whispering and squabbling on the part of *two* of the artistes, and a lot of sleepily contented blinking and obvious satisfaction with his newfound status as a star, on the part of the third – after all of that, Harriet and I considered ourselves uniquely privileged to be present at the first public performance of The Bombelina Song.

> "Bombles the pretty kitty
>   Had some very cool-cat clothes,
>   And if you got your camera
>   He might even agree to pose..."

"We didn't make up the tune," admitted Naomi at the end, rather modestly, following several more verses and two whole encores and a load of hugs and congratulations and tickles and Smarties (well, the three we found left at the bottom of one of the tubes; somehow they'd got stuck there) and also following – well, appropriately enough – the taking of four or five photographs.

"You didn't make up the tune? No, I think we realized that."

But then I added:

48

"How about 'he might even *deign* to pose' – wouldn't that be better?"

I informed them of the spelling, and of the way this new word mightn't be completely the right one, since it imparted an air of condescension to the still very unpretentious Bombles – utterly unspoilt, despite his enjoyment of an overnight fame which might well have turned all lesser heads.

"Remember it till bedtime and we'll give you double what we owe."

# 15

"Now will you trust me?"

I told him I would do my very best.

He paused; seemed satisfied. "And in view of that over-riding interest which I take in Christmas...are you beginning to form any vague suspicions yet?"

"About what? About what, I mean, in *particular*?"

"Who my boss is."

"Oh, yes... The President of Stars," I answered, cannily.

He grinned. "Alias?"

"Alias Santa Claus," I said.

I thought I was being funny again but he seemed to take me seriously. "Or in other words – St Nicholas? Yes. Well done."

All right. My whole attitude had changed during the past few minutes. I now felt no fear of him at all: this friendly, pleasant-faced young man. And I really wanted to believe in him.

But despite his knowing my every thought, almost before I had even thought it, he plainly wasn't going to make things easy for me. Was he?

I was sitting again. I shifted to the left; then shifted to the right. Found I couldn't meet his eye.

"Yep." He nodded, wearily. "The reaction of almost every adult in the world.    But that's what Odin works for. Night and day he works for it."

Well, yes, that may be so. But why should you imagine *my*

reaction would be different?

"Because *I'm* here," he said. "And I banked on your being able to sense I was reliable."

Okay, but why me? Me? I'm eighty-three years old. I'm tired. Spent. A has-been. Without much hope. Or faith. Or dignity. And yet still you come to me and take away my bottle and talk about the stars. And saints. And Santa Claus. And tell me to believe.

"'Why you?'" he said. "That's simple. Well...part of it is simple. You're here because of Odin."

"Then I really wish I'd never met him!"

"Do you?" He paused. He gave me a slow smile. "Well, maybe we'll come back to that. But when you *did* meet him, was he flying through the skies in his golden chariot, with a raven perched on either shoulder?"

"What?"

"Was he wearing his winged helmet; his blue cloak; and wielding his mighty spear?"

"First Santa Claus," I complained, "and now mythology. No, of course he wasn't. I saw him in his office and he was wearing a pinstriped suit. But – hey, just wait a minute! *Ravens*, did you say?"

He gave me another slow smile. He said, "I'm simply pointing out, *en passant*, that this fine friend of yours wasn't always quite so much the boardroom type. He's actually changed a bit, down through the centuries."

I grappled with this new concept: *down through the centuries*.

He added: "Which is why STARS came into being."

Oh, for heaven's sake. Again! *Everybody* knew that those tiresome stars had been there forever. Had been there, indeed, since the beginning of time.

"Society to Abolish Rogue Santas," he said.

"What?"

"It's an acronym, obviously. Society to – "

"I know what an acronym is!"

"Yes. I wasn't suggesting you didn't. It isn't true, though, is it? Your claimed dislike of children?"

I said: "Astonishing! Quite astonishing! Your talent for sticking so closely to the subject!"

"What's nearer the mark is this. You simply won't allow yourself to think fondly of children and that's because – "

"Oh, do put a sock in it! I beg of you! Can't you *please* put a sock in it?"

"But, Richard, admit it – aren't I right?"

"*Stop* it!" I had suddenly realized something: I was a free agent. And I now made to stand up. "There's no reason whatever I must stay here to listen to this."

"No, that's true," he replied. "There isn't a thing to prevent you from leaving this place. Or else from telling *me* to leave it. And now...if I knew you were fully aware of what you were saying...I should have to go."

Maybe as much as a minute went by.

I sank back onto my chair.

He went on standing by the counter, leaning against it with arms and ankles crossed. His favourite stance.

I said: "I expect you think you're very clever, don't you?"

"No. All I think is...well, if I hadn't grown a bit wiser, given the way things are, it would not simply be sad but also quite remarkable. Oh, come on, Dick. It isn't any sign of weakness, you know: the fact that it still hurts. Won't you give me the go-ahead, simply by *admitting* it?"

His tone grew even more cajoling.

"And it wouldn't take more than just a few seconds."

I turned my back on him. Fought back the tears. Clenched my fists; dug my fingernails into my palms.

"Then blast you! Oh, blast you! *Yes*! Children remind me of Peter and Naomi. There! Does that make you any happier?"

"Much. What ages would they both be now?"

I couldn't bring myself to answer.

"And by the way, Dick, it wasn't your fault, you know. It was not your fault."

"I would have died for them," I said.

"I realize that."

"Oh, God. If only it could have been me, not them. Hardly turned eight...nine. Their lives not yet beginning... How can life be so unfair?"

"I don't know."

"And Harriet, as well. Harriet, as well." I said suddenly: "*Why* don't you know?"

But I didn't give him time to tell me.

"She, too, was only young. Why *her*, not me? She was so much nicer than I am. And anyway, in the end, she'd have been able to cope with things far better – far, *far* better... I thought you claimed you had grown wise."

"Though not enough. Not nearly enough. It all takes time," he said.

"Then how long before you *will* know? Just tell me that!" With my eyes now dry, I felt I could at last turn round.

And as I did so, I suddenly found myself staring at him. All at once, the truth had become so glaringly transparent.

"I mean, how long have you been...? How long have you been...?"

"Yes, Dick, you *can* say it. I promise you. It's perfectly all right to say it."

"Because you are, aren't you? You're...dead."

# 16

Perhaps I should have been frightened, or at least uncomfortable. In fact, I felt neither.

"Yes, I am dead." He smiled. "But, before anything else, I want you to know that Harriet, Peter and Naomi all send their love. And their love for you is every bit as strong and abiding as yours for them."

He had to repeat what he'd said – repeat it, in one form or another, half a dozen times.

"And they're happy?"

"*Happy*? Happier in the main than anyone alive could possibly imagine."

"And tell me how they look."

"Beautiful. Resplendent. Forever in their prime."

"They're in their prime?"

"Naturally. We all are." He paused; then laughed. "And yes, Dick, of course you're going to recognize them."

"Oh, dear heaven. This is wonderful."

"Which brings us back to Christmas."

"It does?"

"Which also should be wonderful. Full of wonder."

But for the moment I had other things to think about, infinitely more absorbing. "And you see, we'd probably have had grandchildren by now, even great-grandchildren...and they could've been like any of these kids who've...and they really do talk about me, like you say, and care about me and forgive...?"

"I swear to you, I wouldn't lie."

"No, I know you wouldn't. Yet I didn't think things could ever be this good again. Oh, nothing like it! And I'm sorry if I'm running on but you've got no idea how long it is since...and I've really missed her so."

"You run on as much as you like, Dick."

"But – Christmas, now – you wanted to talk about Christmas? Whatever you ask, I'll do it, Bill. You did say it was Bill, didn't you? It's funny but you look familiar. What is it you were wanting to say about Christmas?"

"It may come as something of a shock."

"What does that matter?"

Didn't he see? I had a family behind me now. My wife and my kids.

Of course, I'd have to clean myself up a bit. A *bit*? I'd have to learn to regulate the booze. I'd have to find a way to earn my keep. (Submit articles to magazines and newspapers, maybe? In the old days, as a hobby, I had often tried to write things.)

Find some way of making them feel just a little bit proud of me.

Nothing could hurt me any more. *Nothing*!

# 17

"It may come as something of a shock," he'd said. And despite the fact I'd thought I could never be thrown by anything again – not ever, *ever* again – still, I suppose, to be quite truthful, I do have to admit it, I *was* thrown. It did come as something of a shock.

"Wage war on Odin?" I cried. "War? On Odin? But dear sweet heaven! *How*?"

"To be honest, Dick, we don't know. All we do know: a chance will certainly turn up tonight and every chance needs to be taken. Even though" (but it seemed he added this more to himself than to me) "we're still extremely weak…" He was frowning a little, and I felt he was having to make a real effort to regain his equanimity. "Whenever we fail to beat him back, the enemy grows stronger."

I wasn't even clear how Odin had become the enemy.

"Earlier on," he said, "you used the word 'mythology'. In Norse mythology Odin was a god. Wholly selfless; wholly good."

"In what way, good?"

"Well – for example – he allowed one of his eyes to be gouged out and let himself be strung up from an oak tree, over three full days, in exchange for wisdom and a knowledge of runes, which he sincerely hoped would benefit mankind."

I didn't know what runes were, either.

"Letters of an ancient alphabet: used in the preparation of spells."

But that was a digression.

"Benefit mankind!" I repeated, ironically. "Didn't something go a little wrong there?"

"Yes. He very clearly overdid things." But in Bill's tone there wasn't any trace of irony; I felt ashamed. "His mind was gradually affected. Not that this became apparent till long after St Nicholas had begun his work among the poor. You see, Odin had always been extremely popular – and particularly so with children."

I wondered why; but didn't want to interrupt.

"Well, apart from anything else, he owned the fastest horse in the world – a horse that had eight legs and could gallop over mountains and sea. It drew his golden chariot...and children thought this plain terrific. It made him splendid and heroic: literally, someone to look up to. But, of course, it made him less accessible."

Forgetfully, I wiped my nose on the back of my mitten, then wiped the mitten down my overcoat, just when I'd been meaning to start working on my manners, restore them to the way they'd been.

"Whereas Nicholas, who was ministering largely to homeless youngsters, the sort society really didn't want to know about...Nicholas was amazingly approachable. Small wonder, then, he should have grown to be the favourite – though he probably never gave this any thought. Even after he'd been made the patron saint of children he still guessed nothing about the feelings of his rival."

"Didn't realize any rivalry had grown?"

"That's right," said Bill. "But things got worse as St Nick grew more and more associated with Christmas. Soon nobody remembered Odin. And after that – so far as Odin was concerned – the name of the game had now become revenge."

I sighed. "Yet that was all so long ago! Surely?"

"Not really. Time's relative. If you think back to ancient Scandinavia, then Christmas still seems new, Santa Claus much newer. Quite *recent* developments, in fact, in the world's long evolution. But even more than that..."

"Yes?"

"Scolopendrid," he said.

"Where?" I wheeled about in agitation.

"No. Don't be alarmed. I only mean that before Scolopendrid showed up, it wasn't yet the right time. Odin knew instinctively his work required a certain person...one whom he'd instantly recognize, however long he had to wait. But then – at last – his spies brought him back word of Scolopendrid! Incredible scoop! And Scolopendrid has proved so much the person Odin was hoping for that they're almost like father and son. It would be touching if it weren't so tragic."

At least I now understood why Odin had chosen Hagalaz & Son as his base of operations.

"Yes," corroborated Bill, "virtually any large store in London or New York would otherwise have done."

"But what I still don't grasp...how a single toy department...either in London or New York or in any other city of the world..."

"Dick, let me give you a small example – except that, in fact, it really *isn't* so small. No, far from it. None of the toys you see around you here is actually for sale. The toys which customers take home are duplicates. Well, almost duplicates. They possess one crucial difference."

I remembered the sales assistant who'd been balled out by Mr Daglock and then later, though still only on my first day, been fired by Mr Chugglefroth – apparently the one immediately over Daglock, in the Hagalaz oligarchy. I remembered how the incident had made me laugh. And they *tell* you that old men no longer blush!

Bill jumped down from the counter. He'd been sitting on it for a while.

"Those duplicates are designed to fall apart within an hour of being unwrapped," he said. His expression was growing grimmer by the instant. "So what inevitably follows? Disappointment, frustration, misery. For the parents as well as the children. A double reason for the enemy to celebrate."

I felt relief. Of course what I'd heard wasn't very nice but it wasn't nearly as frightening as it might have been. "Don't the parents simply return, then, and claim a refund?"

"And what if they do? The damage has been done...Christmas ruined, attitudes altered!" He rubbed his eyes wearily. I'd never thought of a ghost as needing to rub his eyes; perhaps it was only whilst ghosts were *being* ghosts that they reverted to earthly habits. "Merely the most cynical and *Scrooge*-like influences, or vibes, are going to be handed down from now on. Vibes affecting everything – not purely Christmas. Handed down through every generation. Unending," he said, morosely.

I hardly knew what put the notion in my head. "The runes!" I exclaimed.

"Yes. Absolutely. Runes that cause disillusion and enduring memories of resentment. Plus a further runic feature: the ability to shape the feelings of the parents. They'll at once conclude the breakage was due solely to their children's clumsiness and ingratitude – to their indifference to expense. Relatively few of them will even come back to request a refund."

He added:

"And only imagine, Dick, just how this virulence is going to spread if such a pattern continues for another ten or twenty years in department stores across the globe. And make no mistake about it. It will continue. Irreversibly. Unless, of course..."

"Yes?"

"Unless we can somehow put an end to it."

I had an awful feeling that by 'we' he might be meaning 'you'.

He said: "I'm dead, remember. The dead can't change the course of history. Not directly. Not even St Nicholas can change the course of history."

There was perhaps a crumb of consolation to be picked up here. "Then Odin can't, either?"

"No," said Bill. "Like us, he must depend on volunteers."

My brain hadn't seemed so active in ages. "But stop! Hang on a moment..."

I saw him raise an eyebrow.

"You're suggesting that ghosts, the non-living, can't do anything that's in any way concrete? Then how about your trick with my bottle of Scotch?" I looked up at the ceiling, where I expected to see it still floating.

But it wasn't there!

He laughed. "You know, I was wondering if we'd ever get back to that. But all I did, you see, was use telepathy to pop a certain idea into your head. 'Supposing this madman were to whisk the bottle out of my hand and send it flying off magically to the ceiling...?' Your overwrought imagination immediately seized on that."

"But, surely, if you can use telepathy...?"

He shrugged. "What use is telepathy without a willing volunteer? Someone to act out our intentions? Someone alive, who can *indeed* change the course of history?"

So my bottle was still on terra firma…thank goodness! (That last bit was purely automatic.)

"Yet why tonight?" I asked. "You could've come and said all this to me three weeks ago. Why not? I'd have broken all the toys in the stockroom! I'd have cleaned up my act in the grotto! Maybe hundreds of Christmases might have been saved by that…"

"Not hundreds. Thousands," he murmured, gloomily.

"Well, then? My point exactly."

But I'd forgotten, of course, the power they exerted. The bracelet: always keeping me in check. The whisky: always clouding my judgment. The constant supervision: destroying my initiative.

"However," he said. "Please believe this, Dick. There's a proper time for everything. For ourselves quite as much as for Odin."

"But why should tonight, in particular, be the proper time? Tonight and not three weeks ago? How can you tell?"

"Christmas Eve," he said.

He saw my vacant look.

"Listen. For two thousand years now, things have been thought to stir abroad on Christmas Eve. Strange things; malignant things. Witches, trolls, vampires. Zombies, hobgoblins." He produced a faint smile. "And on the very rare occasion…or so they try to tell me…even a ghost or two."

I found none of this particularly encouraging.

"Yet then there are also certain trees which are known both to bloom and to fruit on this especial night. Animals may be blessed with speech; bees may sing; cattle kneel, and sheep take part in ritual. Even Shakespeare says that in the season around Christmas 'the nights are wholesome'. I think that comes from *Hamlet*."

"But *Hamlet* wasn't set in Hagalaz & Son."

"True. Yet here's another quote. 'Be still then, and know that I am God.'"

I felt embarrassed; made no answer. He gave me roughly half a minute in which to ponder his quotation.

Later, I could hardly believe I hadn't put to him all *sorts* of questions.

"Now," he said. "Tell me everything you can about Park Lane."

"Excuse me?"

"About Odin's office in Park Lane."

I really found it hard to readjust. "Which doesn't exist any more," I answered, dully.

"That's complex. Let's merely say that Odin can't ever take a step outside it – although he badly needs to travel. Just tell me of your visit there."

"You aren't already intimate with every detail?"

A small return to irony...although not quite, I think, to sarcasm.

He shook his head – tolerantly. "It's hugely frustrating," he said, "but *their* technology runs neck-and-neck with ours. Which means that certain places exist where we've never been able to watch what goes on. Amongst them, Park Lane and, also, the grotto here. So whatever information you can supply us with, Dick...well, you literally can't imagine how helpful we might find it."

I made a grimace. "Information from a rogue Santa? My, my! That must be a turn-up for the book?"

But he treated my comment seriously.

"Yes, well...rogue Santas," he said. "Since the very *first* Santa Claus – whom you'd have found in America at the start of the last century – there've always been a few who cared for nothing but the money. On the other hand, however, there have always been hundreds who were excellent. But none...not one of them...has ever been in the position that you are in tonight – in a position, quite possibly, to save us."

"Hmm," I said. Disbelievingly.

"No, Dick, I'm not exaggerating. *To save us!*" he repeated.

Then he added:

"So now, whatever you do, stop feeling guilty, please. The past is past. And henceforth the only thing that truly matters..."

Fleetingly, I thought about the future. It felt like a bit of a novelty, doing that.

"Okay. But for the moment I just want to hear about your visit to Park Lane," he reminded me, smiling.

At first, I thought that – after so much time and so much whisky – I shouldn't be able to recall it very clearly. In fact, I really surprised myself.

No. I really shocked myself.

*

For I found that what I most vividly remembered was a whole section of the interview which – previously – I hadn't even been aware of.

So why not? Could I have been hypnotized? Spellbound? And, in that case, why were the effects of this only now beginning to lose their potency? Could it possibly be because…well, because the nights *are* wholesome around Christmas?

In any event, I went straight back into it: that visit to Park Lane.

# 18

"Can't I help you out?"

"Oh, Rich. How deeply your simple goodness does affect me."

And, sure enough, he had to turn his head away, to conceal the full extent of his emotion.

Six of his secretaries came in then…or, rather, I was suddenly aware of their presence. I saw them dabbing at their eyes in unison, to show how much the boss's powerful feelings were shared by his employees.

"But I think you'll find I'm not ungrateful," said Lord Odin, when sufficiently recovered. "Not only shall I make sure you're abundantly supplied with the tipple I can see you're very fond of;

I shall also strain to devise many other methods of rewarding you. Dear Rich, you'll find you can rely on my loving-kindness and ingenuity."

I wondered if he meant wages. Perhaps he thought it wouldn't be good form to say so.

"And indeed," he continued, "even becoming a Santa Claus for a short spell needn't be unrelievedly grim. There may be certain ways of enlivening it."

"I can't imagine how."

Then at once, as if they'd all been eagerly awaiting this, the secretaries cried out in supplication. "Oh, yes, Lord, won't you tell us how?"

His Lordship removed his feet from the desktop and began consideringly to pace the office, stroking that fine cleft chin as he did so, that strong determined jaw.

"Well...hmm...let me see. I've never given it a second's thought. But let me see...I need to have a little time...ah, yes, I do believe I've got it! Probably not worth a mention but you must tell me how it comes across to you."

"Oh, wonderfully!" exclaimed his secretaries; and no one but me seemed to consider this a trifle premature.

Lord Odin delivered his pronouncements.

"Rich, don't ever wash during the period of your Santaship; the smellier you can get to be...the more tightly you can hug those precious little darlings..."

The secretaries, both men and women, all pulled hankies from their breast pockets and waved them fastidiously before their faces. "Oh...my! That delicate aroma of stale sweat. How much they're going to love it! That subtle scent of spirits on the breath – of garlic and tobacco. How much it will delight them!"

Odin nodded approvingly; and turned from them to me. "Yes – and, of course, you'll yawn a lot. Full in their trusting little faces."

The chorus said, "Oh, heavenly. Heavenly. We find this so uplifting."

Odin held up a gentle, warning finger. "But, naturally, you'll quickly make it clear this isn't merely because you're tired. You're also very bored."

Obedient to a man, or woman, the secretaries each yawned prodigiously. "Oh, my, the monotony! Quite soul-destroying! So what's the time *now*, for heaven's sake?" They yawned again and stretched. "And only to think...I could have taken a job in a factory. Fitting nuts onto bolts! All day long! How glorious!"

But there were now two things which had definitely begun to worry me. One was that I'd become aware I wasn't agreeing quite so fully as before. And the other:

"Yet aren't the parents, Lord, going to feel just the slightest bit hesitant? I only mean, sir, would *you* hand over your own sweet-smelling treasure to a person who stunk like me?"

"Oh, good thinking! Good thinking! How splendid, how refreshing it is, finally to come across somebody who has a brain! But have no fear, my dearest Rich. The parents won't actually see you. They'll hand over that twinkling little treasure to a female who'll appear as feminine as she is fragrant, as protective as she is pretty, as trustworthy as she is tall. Eh, Dorinda? You and your brood of charmingly elongated sisters?" He chuckled; and just a moment later the whole room seemed to be full of quiet, appreciative chuckles. "Yet in case you should ever feel anxious about some other small point...the little treasures themselves are never going to rat on you...you may rest assured of *that*!"

"But how can you possibly be certain?" (It sounded somewhat bald; I hurriedly tacked on, "Lord".)

"Oh, trust me, Rich! I rely so fully on your trust. On your co-operation."

I felt that I had let him down.

"But what was I saying, now? I've lost my whole train of thought. Which is truly not your fault, my dearest friend! No, please don't reproach yourself! Ever! Please!"

He gave me a noble and long-suffering smile.

"Ah...yes... Hadn't we reached that part where you can start to regale all those bright-eyed little darlings, *formerly* bright-eyed little darlings, whom you've now got securely fastened to your side, start to regale them with titbits concerning your dirty, aching feet and your varicose veins and your dentures that keep slipping? (Maybe take the dentures out and show off all those stray bits of spinach you couldn't quite get at before? You can do this fairly casually. Maybe scrape at them with a dead match?) Yes, hadn't we reached that part where you can throw in a few choice references to old folks' ailments, all the time suggesting that such ailments commonly afflict even *young* folks, even twenty-somethings and teenagers? That this is their own inescapable fate, just lurking around some fast-approaching corner. You can improvise, Rich. Yes, naturally. That all contributes vastly to the fun."

I swallowed. Lord Odin was inclined to exaggerate a little. Yes? In the same way that his chorus was? He surely couldn't *quite* be meaning all he said.

Could he?

"But whatever happens (and, Rich, I do so hope you're listening; I realize that at times I can be *such* a bore!), whatever happens, don't waste any of your valuable moments talking about reindeer pulling sleighs or about sacks full of interesting surprises. Oh, no! No talk at all of *that* depressing nature..."

He added more slowly: "Oh, I don't know, though. On the other hand, it might be rather sweet to speak of Santa getting stuck down the chimney – obviously, I mean, some goody-two-shoes kind of Santa. Mmm," he said. "The possibility of suffocation, the hope of someone lighting up a big, fierce, crackling blaze..." His Lordship cast a tantalising glance at the chorus.

And the chorus responded merrily. And musically. Immortalised the moment in a song.

> "Santa roasting on an open fire,
>   Tummy wedged between hot bricks..."

I'd always thought the words had something more to do with chestnuts and jollier forms of Yuletide cheer.

But, anyway, yes. Surely all this had to be a *bit* of an exaggeration? Of course it did!

No good, however. Ensconced there in my low armchair I was beginning actually to squirm. I wasn't enjoying myself.

Or maybe I simply hadn't understood it correctly; had

somehow misread this whole accumulatively alarming situation?

But in any case I judged it would be best merely to express my appreciation for His Lordship's hospitality. Offer him my fervent apologies – my sincere regrets: I'd remembered a most important engagement I must hurry to.

Lord Odin frowned.

It seemed he'd noticed my cigar had gone out.

He snapped his fingers as though this were actually a circumstance to panic over; and one of the repentant secretaries leapt forward – yes, practically *leapt* forward – to put the matter right.

Yet only when the cigar was once more exhaling plumes of blue aromatic smoke did Lord Odin gradually relax again.

"But, Lord..." I faltered. I couldn't think exactly how to phrase it.

"Yes, Rich?" His look was brimming over with understanding and encouragement. "Second thoughts, my dear fellow? Oh, no. You can't possibly wish to tell me you're regretting – oh, please don't tell me you're regretting – your earlier lovely promise to become my friend...to serve me and to call me Lord?"

The secretaries seemed equally solicitous. "Oh, Rich. Can there possibly be something which is causing you concern?"

Lord Odin looked at them laconically.

"Get out," he said.

And out they got. But they went in a high-kicking chorus line, exiting through double doors, hands on each other's shoulders, faces turned to the left, fixed grins big enough to light up all of Broadway.

So I decided to take this as my own cue to depart. Dropping my cigar butt into the remains of my Scotch (although if I hadn't been in such a rush, no way would I have thought of leaving even those) I heard it fizz rebelliously. I quickly set the tumbler on the floor; forgot about flicking the ash off my overcoat; and tried to rise.

But, like I've said, the chair was low and before I could manage to do so, Lord Odin had moved across to where I sat.

"Rich, my foolish man, won't you only *tell* me what the matter is? I feel so sure that – between us – we can swiftly work things out."

He warmly gripped my hand. I noticed the cloying scent of his cologne. He looked at me sympathetically with his bright blue, ever-watchful eye.

Yet what had happened next?

My left-hand sleeve...

# 19

Bill scrutinized the bracelet. "You know what we could really do with?" he suggested. "A laser!"

"Well, perhaps Mrs Whipplecrump...?" Sarcasm dies hard. "In amongst her other cleaning things...?"

"But it's not troubling you at the moment?"

I paused. "No. I don't think I've felt it since you told me about Harriet. About Harriet and the children!"

"And you cried," he said.

"Yes? Well? What does that have to do with it?"

"And you put your hand to your eyes; you wiped your nose on your sleeve..." He gazed at me excitedly. "Don't you understand? Your *tears* could have touched the bracelet!"

"So?"

"Tears! Sorrow! The solvent of remorse!" He punched the palm of his hand. "Yes, say a prayer, Dick, we're going to try it!"

However, there remained one snag. You can't cry remorseful tears just because it's been suggested. They have to be sincere, spontaneous. I still had plenty to regret – oh, plenty, *plenty*! – but even so...

"Take off your glove!" he told me.

I did so.

"Am I imagining this," he asked, "or does it really feel damp?"

Well, if *he* was imagining it, then *I* was, too.

65

His voice became a lot softer. It wasn't so much as if he feared being overheard, more as if he sensed some quality in the air which he felt nervous of disturbing.

"Now find the part that's dampest. Then wrap it round the bracelet. As tightly as you can...with every ounce of energy you have."

So I selected what seemed the wettest patch in all the wool. And at precisely that moment we saw a dark green pulse beating below the surface of the stone. Beating, I was sure, in panic.

"Now – *pray*!" urged Bill.

I prayed.

"And don't merely *ask* for a miracle. Believe with all your heart that it's about to happen!"

Easier said than done. (Because it still hadn't fully sunk in – that incredibly joyous revelation I'd received only a short time earlier.) "Yes, yes!" I cried. "*Yes*!"

"Now it's working loose, isn't it?"

Perhaps it was? Perhaps it truly was?

Then suddenly a brutal stab shot through my wrist – a stab as bad as any I had yet experienced. I forgot everything but my desire to neutralize that pain. And miracles be blowed! – I waved my arms like I was beating out a fire. Brought down my fists like I was killing bedbugs. Lunged at the air like I was knifing demons in the gut.

And it worked! It worked! The flames were extinguished, the bedbugs squashed, the demons good and gutted. The bracelet spun away from me. Hit the floor with a clunk – accompanied by a prolonged metallic screech.

Then it flashed and sizzled as it rolled towards a dark periphery. Possibly the pain was still inside it, trying desperately to spit its sharp way out. I caught a smell of burning dust. (Oh, Mrs Whipplecrump!) Its weakening glow grew duller by the instant.

Duller. Darker. Then faded altogether. The bracelet, bereft of glow, became nothing more than a smudge in the shadow.

My wrist was swollen – deeply grooved and ringed with red.

But it was free. *Free.*

"Thank you," I said – oh, words can be so helplessly inadequate! Bill nodded. He murmured that anyway it wasn't him I had to thank; but his slightly automatic smile, indeed his whole reaction, lacked much of the exuberance I'd have expected.

"Just in time," he whispered.

"Why?"

"Well, don't you see?"

"See what? Where? What d'you mean?"

"Santa's Castle of Snow," he snapped. "Can't you see what's happening?" He added in an undertone: "*Santa's*, my foot!"

I looked at the castle. The corner that it occupied was some fifty, sixty yards away – and in the gloom of the department I really had to strain my eyes.

Which suddenly seemed peculiar. Throughout the past three weeks the castle had provided a landmark in the dark. Normally its very whiteness rendered it luminescent. Like a swarm of fireflies roosting in a tree. You always knew that it was there.

"It's melting," murmured Bill.

"Melting?" I thought that I'd misheard. If anything the castle's outline – though indistinct – was larger than before. More imposing. Appeared to be taking up more space.

Which patently couldn't have been possible.

"The snow!" he said. "It's casting off its snow!"

"Oh, surely? Can't be!"

"The snow is only camouflage."

I peered at it with still more concentration; shambled a few feet nearer...while obviously taking care not to impose too much of a distance between myself and my companion.

I gasped.

"Bill! Oh, strewth. Dear God! It's changing shape."

"Yes."

"*And* growing bigger!"

"Yes."

I remembered it as Disneyesque: all graceful turrets, crazily elegant, an iced-cake kind of palace, the dream of some eccentric kaiser. Now it was beginning to resemble a fortress: less fancy – more functional. No longer out of a silly symphony by Walt

Disney. Now featuring in a solid novel by Sir Walter Scott. A novel set during the Middle Ages.

Armies and attackers. Battle cries. Grappling irons.

Ladders.

Pitchers of boiling oil... I moved back a little closer to Bill.

A moon seemed to have come out. The castle now had battlements and a portcullis and a drawbridge. It had slits through which to rain down arrows. It had walls that looked a foot thick.

But what did I mean: *now* it had these things? I shuddered; was about to demand a reassuring explanation. A stirring rose behind us. Our heads jerked round in dismay.

It was like a series of soft movements...hard to pinpoint just at first...as when you open your eyes in a dosshouse in the dark: there's always somebody slowly turning over, or else scratching, or snoring, or wheezing, or stumbling up to go to the loo – always signs of reanimating life. But you can't quite put a name to each individual movement and you often don't know, precisely, what it was that woke you.

Well, so it was in this case. While I stood beside Bill, awake yet shell-shocked and all at sea, the initial faint stirrings took long, fathomless seconds in which to disentangle themselves.

But bit by bit there emerged sounds you could identify, shapes you could begin to recognize.

And these shapes were marching on the castle.

Moreover – while they went marching past us – they commenced to sing.

"Men of Odin, band together,
Men of Odin, flags unfurled,
Men of Odin, true forever,
Men of Odin, rule the world!"

They still weren't easy to see but they conveyed an air of collective strength and didn't appear – no, not in the slightest – like toys who'd been timed to fall apart. (Or, if they *were* so timed, you knew the headsman's axe would implant itself in your neck as it was falling; the boa constrictor – in the long minutes

68

before it disintegrated – would wind lethally around your waist; the bear would squeeze you lifeless to the tune of its own death rattle.) And they all seemed to have grown on a scale to match the castle. One Barbie doll turned eyes on me that looked like some Amazonian warrior's. Her sister was Lucrezia Borgia. In each one's aspect, apparent even through the twilit shadows, existed deadliness combined with cuteness...like blowpipes lifted to mouths all freshly lipsticked and dabbed upon pink tissue. This cuteness was probably what enthralled the two ragged, sunburnt adventurers who followed leeringly in their wake; also the sharp-shooting Mexican bandit and the Chinese warlord who were marching in tidy crocodile immediately behind *them*.

These and maybe some thirty others – the entire procession being led by the bear and an immense black widow spider – made up a queer and motley crew. But they had one irrefutable thing in common: a look of resentment, a look of self-seeking and defiant hardness, a look that said, "Stand aside, please; we mean to reach the top and nothing's going to stop us!" Their march, their chant, their whole arrogant demeanour, bore striking witness to this fact. "Ah, you poor pathetic saps," they might have smiled. "So you suppose we're simple stockroom replicas – is that what you think? Fine! Then why not just continue to suppose it...that is, so long as you still possess the means, sweet innocents, of supposing anything at all?"

And while we watched, they crawled, or slid, or clattered over the drawbridge. True to their song, many of them carried flags. As the drawbridge was raised, and the portcullis lowered, their words grew less distinct, muffled by the thickness of the stone. I saw moonlight gleaming on a moat, heard water lapping against ramparts. Two ravens soared above the battlements.

"Well, now," said Bill, "wouldn't you know it – our dear old friends, Hugin and Mugin?"

"Could they hurt me?" Tonight, indeed, they looked particularly fearsome; perhaps because – although the ceilings were high and the department extensive – I hadn't yet encountered them within an enclosed space.

69

"No. They're like the rest of us. They might fly in your face and caw, they might demonstrate their wing span, but they can't do more than merely frighten."

*Merely*, I thought. "Then why are they so restless?" One of them had now landed and was hopping from crenellation to crenellation. I remembered how ultra-motionless they'd both appeared, perched on the railings of that balcony in Park Lane. Silent. A pair of statuettes.

"They're restless because it's Christmas Eve and their reporting has to be wholly without mistake."

"Reporting to Odin?"

I wondered where he was now. Odin. From the world outside the store, only darkness pressed against the windows. (At least, what passed for darkness in any place like Oxford Street.) I almost found it hard to imagine there still *was* a world outside the store: a world in which people were simply getting on with their lives and doing normal things…like cooking, seeing to last-minute chores, adding some final touches to the tree. Many watching the box; leaving the cinema; travelling on the tube. Perhaps sinking a pint or two inside their local. And others of course, at around this time, preparing to go to Midnight Mass.

Yes, I was glad to have remembered. It felt reassuring. All of it.

But Bill was staring at the ravens and not looking in the least reassured. "Isn't it easy enough to imagine they were once the eyes and ears of King Henry VIII and instrumental in bringing all sorts of suspects – including two of the king's own wives – first to the Traitor's Gate and then to the executioner's block? Oh, how they would have relished it: watching the results of their efficiency from an elm branch on Tower Hill, having their own comfy seats at the ringside! And it was probably them, Dick, who organized that small show of strength just now – which of course was nothing but the purest bluff and bluster," he added, immediately. "We're both *very* well aware of that. Aren't we?"

Yet, unfortunately, what I felt very well aware of was that Bill was only trying to play things down. That singing and banner-waving parade of highly nasty-looking individuals…mere

70

bluff and bluster? No, surely not. 'Intimidation tactics' was more the phrase *I* might have used. And undeniably successful ones. *So* successful I was suffering a relapse. "Dear God," I was asking, "won't you please get me out of here? I'm just a fellow who was looking for a few free drinks; hardly your typical have-a-go hero! Of what possible use could *I* ever be?"

But then Bill gave me a further instruction which seemed to have no relevance whatever.

"Dick, for a moment," he said, "just think back to the war."

"The war?"

"October, 1941. You were on leave, remember? You were passing a bombed-out building. You thought you heard a moan."

Oddly enough, I *did* remember.

"And although people insisted you were only dreaming – that everyone had been brought out – you kept on tearing at those mounds of rubble, like no power on earth could ever stop you."

Now, suddenly, I realized what was coming. From the start I had thought he looked familiar.

"That man you found...he died only *minutes* later. You were holding onto his hand and pleading with him not to go. Just to hang on."

I said: "It was as if I'd lost a friend."

"Then can you wonder I should take so strong an interest in you? That my parents should take so strong an interest in you? That lots of others should, as well?"

At some point he had put his arm around my shoulders. I only became aware of this as he took the arm away.

"Dick, I've got to leave."

I panicked again. Right there, on the spot.

"Got to leave? But why? *Why*?"

"Because – whatever happens – you need to face this on your own."

"*Why*?" I must have sounded like a child.

Bill must have sounded like a parent.

"Don't you see, Dick? Fifty years ago you could rely upon yourself. And others could rely on you. You had your dignity, your self-respect. It's got to be that way again."

"Oh, no, Bill! Why has it? Oh, hang my dignity – my self-respect! It's the STARS you should be thinking of. What's best for Christmas and the STARS."

"But your becoming well again...it's all a part of it. Our work is nothing if it's not about the individual – the individual quite as much as the crowd. And we *know* you've got it in you!" He smiled and shook his head. "This is no time to hang up your spurs, Mr Semple!"

He added quickly:

"Now let me take you across to Blitzen."

Well, how could I refuse? How could friendship, or conscience, or courtesy – or *anything* – allow me to refuse? And in fact it wasn't only to Blitzen I found myself being made known.

Bill beckoned others from their various shelves and stands in the department to come forward to meet me. Up until this point they had seemed to be mere commodities, lifelessly awaiting purchase. (Apparently unaware it was only their *replicas* that would be purchased.) Now, however, they were turning into perceptibly animated creatures, at the precise moment Bill invited each one to approach. "Dick, these are the characters who'll make up the platoon *you* will be commanding."

And, as they presented themselves, I discovered one remarkable feature they had in common: the sheer pleasantness of their expressions. Yes, everybody's – even the crocodile's and the pirate chief's, even the boxing champ's and the whirling dervish's (when he was ever sufficiently still, that was, for anyone to notice). Admittedly, the tempestuous young gypsy whom I instantly recognized as Esmeralda – from *The Hunchback of Notre Dame* – had eyes that were flashing a good deal. But not with cruelty: only in reaction to the cruelty she'd recently observed – right there, on the arrogant faces of the enemy, during its swaggering march-past. No, when she wasn't angry (I was told) her eyes could be every bit as soft as Blitzen's...well, practically so, at any rate.

Yet of all the characters in the department, whether on our own side or on Odin's, Blitzen was the only one who hadn't actually grown – because he had been life-sized to begin with. And now I turned to Bill to comment on this.

72

But Bill wasn't there.

"No! Wait a minute! Stop! Where are you?" I cried.

No movement. Nothing. No yearned-for glimmer of light spilling out from behind some pillar or stand. My call remained unanswered.

*Bill wasn't there*!

# 20

I felt alone; abandoned. The gypsy, the boxer, the buccaneer, all the others, had now resumed their normal sizes, had returned to where they'd come from. Probably done so while I'd been looking around for Bill. *Probably?* You see, I had suddenly thought this whole crazy episode – yes, even this whole crazy three- week episode – might just have been a dream. Everyone has weird dreams: seemingly real at the time but wholly ridiculous afterwards.

Yet to think along such lines made me feel…well, not simply abandoned…bereft. Despite the escalating menace, despite my fluctuating fears, I told myself that if it *had* only been a dream I might really need to throw myself beneath a bus. Once and for all. What would be left?

No Harriet…

No Peter, no Naomi…

No Bill.

No sense of purpose marvellously renewed.

So you see? It couldn't – absolutely couldn't – could *not* have been a dream!

The answer was simple, though. Blitzen wasn't far away.

"Blitzen. I was meaning to ask you..." It didn't matter what. "Where are Dasher and Dancer and Vixen and all the rest?"

In other words: let me know I'm in my right mind. Open your mouth and speak to me in English and tell me I'm in danger.

Please. I want so much to be in danger.

"Anybody's guess," he said.

I could have hugged him; planted a kiss on his cold, damp nose. For even then a surprisingly obvious fact was still escaping me. That if I *had* just woken from a deep sleep, I think I should hardly have been wandering around a department store, apparently on my own and in the middle of the night.

I mean...unlikely, isn't it?

But anyhow.

Blitzen was expanding on his answer. "Do you honestly think a place like this would care about keeping the eight of us together?" Earlier, with Bill, he hadn't sounded half so mournful.

So I did what I could to raise his spirits.

"But in an hour or two you'll all be pulling Santa's sleigh. That's tradition, isn't it? *Nobody* can stop you."

Unless maybe, I reflected glumly, he happens to be called Odin. I decided to shift the emphasis.

"Strewth! It must be mind-blowing to fly. To have all those breathtaking views and that tremendous sense of freedom."

He agreed that it was, yet did so without sounding much happier. "Wish I'd appreciated it, though, while I was still allowed to do it. What I've learned is, you only start to appreciate things when they aren't there any longer."

Oh, Blitzen! *Don't*!

"But you speak as if you'll never fly again," I said.

"Well, I don't suppose I ever shall. Only two ways in which I could: attached to Santa's sleigh, or ridden by an adult human being who really does believe in the powers of enchantment. And as you can imagine...in my experience, you don't come across too many of *those* on an average day. Unfortunately, not everyone is like you, Mr Semple."

*Unfortunately, not everyone is like you, Mr Semple*!

"Then maybe I could help?" I must have spoken without thinking.

He perked up at once; shook his antlers and mane as though invigorated by a sudden burst of sunshine on a rainy day.

"Because very possibly," I went on hurriedly, "when this whole beastly thing is over..."

He drooped again.

74

"Oh, I thought you meant *now*," he murmured. "When this whole beastly thing is over we could all of us be dead."

"Blitzen, how can you say that? How can you even *think* it?"

His response didn't entirely answer my question. "I'd reckoned a moonlit flight might really have restored me."

'Moonlit flight' sounded awfully much like 'moonlight flit'. Actually, at first, that's what I thought he'd said.

"But we haven't got time," I protested. Uncertainly.

"Why not, Mr Semple? Twenty minutes, half an hour? The waiting's always the worst part, anyhow. And nothing's going to happen here before eleven."

"If anything's going to happen here at all..." (Trying to boost my own confidence, quite as much as his.) I added quickly, as the rest of his sentence registered: "But why do you say that: not before eleven?"

Blitzen looked surprised. "Because isn't midnight known to be the witching hour? And, therefore, only the sixty minutes on either side of it can ever be drawn up into witchery."

"Oh... Right... I see what you mean. So if that's the case, why was Bill in such a rush to leave?"

"I don't know. But you can depend on it, Mr Semple, he had his reasons."

"Besides...," I said. Blitzen might have disposed of one of my objections, yet there was definitely another.

"How would we ever get out of here?"

"Oh, no problem over *that*!" he replied.

He made it sound so simple. I didn't want to show my ignorance a second time.

And, all the while, he gazed at me imploringly. Rubbed his nose against my shoulder. Needless to say, those liquid brown eyes of his weren't all that easy to resist.

But I felt I had to justify my fearfulness. Not only to him. To both of us.

"Oh, I wish I were young and adventurous! I wish that I were only twenty-five again..."

His look was understandably reproachful. "It's not how old you are, Mr Semple. It's how your attitude is. Have you any idea what age *I* am?"

Oh, he was right, of course! I'd been behaving like a coward.

What's more, I'd been thinking only of myself, despite my implicit new resolution to do otherwise.

*Unfortunately, not everyone is like you, Mr Semple.*

No. One point was blatantly apparent. Blitzen really needed this journey.

"You've got a passenger!" I said.

# 21

He was touching in his gratitude. "Then climb aboard, Mr Semple!"

Huh! So easy to say. But only when he sank to his knees was I able to accomplish it.

And then – once he was upright – I had my balance to consider. I held onto his antlers for dear life.

After that, moreover, there was a further worry: travel sickness? Nonsense! I hadn't been travelsick since childhood. And for heaven's sake! As yet we hadn't even started!

Or so I thought.

But, suddenly, there we were…skimming over the rooftops!

Though how could this be? Back in the department there had been two more floors above us.

Then had Blitzen decided to go the other way – *down*? To run down the escalators in the central atrium? Having somehow arranged for a main door to be left open? Telepathically?

No!

Bunkum!

So had he merely plunged through a window, up *or* down, and paid no heed to shattering glass?

Balderdash!

Impossible! Impossible! All of it, impossible!

And yet...?

("Magic? You always say you don't believe in anything like that." So distinctly could I hear Bill's voice that I didn't even bother to think about it any longer. There was too much else; *far* too much.)

For at first I was leaning forward with my head between Blitzen's antlers, my legs pressed tightly to his flanks. I was shaken by chill and almost hurricane-force gales, which I feared might knock me senseless – no *huge* exaggeration. But shortly I was calmed by a mixed smell of stable and zoo and was suddenly remembering distant days of riding on the Downs. That ease of movement and the rippling, fluid speed; that heady rush of wind…these felt amazingly familiar. And the fact it wasn't turf we were flying over but cold sharp air we were flying *through* didn't seem for very long either alien or frightening. Soon I became a pilot again in the RAF: my posture less hunched, Blitzen's body and antlers providing me with all the framework that I needed. We had now left England, flown across the North Sea and were gliding over realms of glistening snow. Norway...Sweden...Finland...hardly surprising he should have headed straight for home. Who wouldn't, given half a chance? Now there were mountains and fir trees and forests, and I saw a million stars mirrored frostily in lake and fjord. Illuminated maps of the sky spread out below me.

And yet starlight gave way to sunlight in mere minutes…if not seconds! As fast, indeed, as my nervousness had given way to confidence – to enjoyment and excitement. (Even to cockiness! *Just look at me, everyone…no hands*! *Look at ME, everybody*!) And by that time – no longer resistant to letting the air into my mouth – I was often crying out in pure exhilaration. Quite literally crying out!

"Oh, look! That train! That little train winding its way through the valley – can you see it?"

"Oh, Blitzen, there's a ship! Luxury liner. Passengers in deckchairs. Lucky dogs!"

"Why, my goodness! Wind surfers. Sunbathers. Games of volleyball." I didn't even need my specs. "And those kids down there…would you *believe* the size of that sandcastle? And are people *really* eating turkey and plum pudding on the beach?"

Not that I actually supposed Blitzen could hear me – my words were swept away on the slipstream.

But it wasn't just these things. We saw the Vatican City and the Acropolis and the Sphinx; the Taj Mahal and the Great Wall of China. We saw the Grand Canyon and Yosemite National Park – something told me it was that – and what's the name of that building in Chicago which is now one of the tallest in the world? We saw Niagara Falls and the Nile and the Amazon. The Missouri and the Mississippi. The Andes and the Himalayas. We saw them all.

And what colours! Colours as vibrant as those of tropical blooms and exotic fish, of flamboyant birds and butterflies, of undulating plant life on the barrier reefs, of the lagoons and beaches in between. Colours as distinct as the aquamarine of sparkling seas or the deep pink of the Rose Red City or the emerald green of Ireland. The endless yellow of Arabian sands. We saw them all.

Colours as warm as the burnished gold of minarets and palaces; or the cascading sparks of a volcano; or the coppered surface of a lake at sunset. We saw them all.

In less than an hour I'd had a whistle-stop tour of the planet. The holiday of a lifetime.

Lucky dogs? Just passengers in deckchairs on some old, fuddy-duddy, Caribbean cruise? *They*, in fact, might have been shading their eyes and gazing up at the sky and shouting out with altogether more conviction, "Wow, just look at *them*, those lucky dogs!" I felt refreshed, revitalized and half a century younger. Ready to take on each and every one of my commitments. (A moonlight flit, indeed!) So, praise God, did Blitzen. It was almost with eagerness that we set a course for home.

Home?

Did I say *home*?

# 22

I noticed a greenish glow in the distance. It looked beautiful but odd. It wasn't like the normal glow which can come off any big commercial building, made up of street lighting, window displays, anything emanating from within. This was more like a tower of light – eerily unnatural – a tower of light that might have been climbing up to rendezvous with some UFO, or spaceship.

And then I realized that we were making straight for it.

"Blitzen! That isn't Hagalaz & Son!"

"Yes," he said.

"But, no, it can't be!"

The slipstream – since we were now preparing to land – had ceased to give us trouble.

"It is, Mr Semple. I promise you."

I obviously wasn't doubting his powers of navigation – hadn't we just been around the world together? It was clearly my own powers of adjustment which had to be at fault.

We drew closer to the greenish glow. All right, it did have a familiar look: I mean, the edifice illumined by those rays. I remembered it. I did remember it. But I couldn't think from where. A story? Poster? Magazine?

No, not just an illustration from some book, or an image on some hoarding – I was sure I'd seen the real thing. Well...almost sure I'd seen the real thing.

Turrets. Spires. Arched windows.

Gargoyles. Each gargoyle in possession of a Cyclops eye. Each eye roving and piercing. Jealously protecting.

A balcony looking like a monstrous moth. A black moth. Spread-eagled and staked.

And the whole macabre edifice, as spiky as some Venus flytrap, ensnaring for its sustenance the very energy and substance of the night. And therefore ensnaring – for its sustenance – both Blitzen and myself. *Our* very energy, *our* very substance.

At least, that's what it felt like. That's what it really felt like.

"We *have* gone wrong, Blitzen! I remember this place. It's E.Y. Enterprises in Park Lane."

"No, Mr Semple. Hagalaz & Son in Oxford Street."

I said again: "Can't be!"

And yet – true – Odin's building had been slimmer, hadn't it?

Besides, on reflection, those same features had seemed a lot less pronounced, hadn't they? A lot less…grotesque.

But Hagalaz & Son... Try as I might, I couldn't recall the least trace of Gothic. I certainly hadn't noticed that fifth-floor balcony.

"It's the Flying Fortress, Mr Semple. I'm sure you must have heard of it?"

Yet my mind was all over the place. "The Flying Fortress? The Flying Fortress was an aeroplane – used in the Second World War!"

"Not this one." With his antlers he indicated the building now right before us. "Not a plane," he said, "more of a prison. Then obviously you *don't* know of it: the rumour that it searches constantly for other buildings it can infiltrate? Like the cuckoo which lays its eggs in the nests of small songbirds, who then hatch them and rear the offspring. But the Flying Fortress lays *plans*, not eggs. And certain hosts are only too willing to hatch those plans and see them through to their completion. *Evil* hosts – not one scrap like songbirds. Evil hosts hatching evil plans."

I didn't understand.

"Mr Scolopendrid," he told me, "was clearly one such willing host. *Extremely* willing host! In fact, he probably wins the title. *Most* willing host ever!"

I still didn't understand. Hardly one word; not from beginning to end.

For the present, however, there was no further chance to work it out: I became rapidly distracted, because we'd just landed on the balcony – surely, a larger version of that same balcony where I'd once fallen and measured my length along the cold, wet stone? Now, as I awkwardly dismounted – sliding, slithering, off Blitzen's back (for I didn't like to ask him to go down on his knees a second time) – I nearly fell again. When my feet connected with the ground, my legs were shaking, uncontrollably.

"The journey of a lifetime, Blitzen! That was wonderful! Thank you."

Obviously I meant it but I was aware of sounding a bit fulsome. You see, I didn't want him to suppose I was shaking out of anything but stiffness, or that my bilious complexion – I was convinced it must be bilious – was due to anything but that green, unflattering light.

Yet, despite my best efforts, I could easily have wished he had delivered me almost anywhere but there.

Oh, good heavens, yes!

For the thing was... My only option, my only way out, was through that pair of French windows which I clearly remembered as leading into Odin's office, but through which I now saw merely a cash till ('Please Pay Here') and a bicycle and one of those bugle-playing angels still floating stupidly from the ceiling. In other words, not a way out at all. Simply a way in.

So there was absolutely nothing for it but to push open the French windows.

Blitzen gave a gasp.

"Oh, can't you just feel it, Mr Semple?"

"Feel what?"

"That sudden icy *bite* to the air. That sudden big drop in the temperature!"

It was unquestionably cold. Even to people who had flown straight in from the night sky. I tried to pull my overcoat more tightly about me.

"As if," he said, "as if something very wicked was approaching us!" He broke off. "Oh, the time – the time!" he exclaimed. "Oh, look at the time! I *am* sorry!"

I looked up at the clock.

And how stupid that at such a moment I should again be remembering Shakespeare.

> *By the pricking of my thumbs,*
> *Something wicked this way comes.*

# 23

And suddenly...a lightning flash forking down above the castle. Succeeded by a thunder roll. More lightning.

Then a lengthy confusion of discordant sound. Cacophonous. Impossible to list most of its ingredients.

But certainly high up on such a list: the cackling of witches who came swooping past on broomsticks.

And, next, the demented shriek of one of them, as her black skirts were torn – on landing – by the ball and chain dragged by the shackled foot of a convict. She shrieked, then placed two bony fingers underneath his chin, as though she only meant, forgivingly, to pat it. But no. With that one grinning, cooing, salivating gesture...the old crone pulverised him. Reduced him to a spreading mass of powder.

*Warm*, for you could see the curling wisps of steam arising from it.

Then came the screech of her cat, who'd ridden pillion on the broomstick and had quickly sprung down to sniff and lick at those remains, only to be kicked aside (and *how* it screeched, and spat, and caterwauled!) when they were scooped up by another salivating witch and sprinkled, like cornflour, into the simmering contents of her cauldron.

Much of that powder had run through her fingers, however, and left a phosphorescent trail for the outlaws and desperadoes and gun runners who were all ferociously pursuing one another and screaming vengeance as they did so. Even from a distance, I could see the glint of murder in their eyes.

Could see it by the light of the thunderbolts that zigzagged around the battlements. Zigzagged leisurely, it seemed, as if pleasurably deciding on which of these miscreants *first* to electrocute.

Thankfully, though, the storm at last abated. All these apparitions vanished. The night grew quiet. The moon emerged again.

Blitzen was back in his usual place.

My eye was drawn towards the castle. I quickly realized why. The portcullis was being raised, the drawbridge being lowered.

A tall thin figure sauntered out. A real dandy. Jaunty. Debonair.

But suddenly this figure bowed; bowed absolutely double. Looked as if he might be made of rubber: a member of some circus troupe.

At first I couldn't think what he was doing. Had he found a clump of aromatic flowers and simply stuck his nose in it...revelling in a multitude of sniffs? But not at all. I saw he'd merely paused to study his reflection in the moat. It couldn't have been easy – admiring himself by nothing but moonlight – and yet he lovingly adjusted his tie and pushed up one eyebrow with a carefully licked fingertip. Middle finger of his left hand.

In the buttonhole of his pinstriped suit he sported a red carnation. On his face he sported a smile.

I'd vaguely supposed he must be gadding off to one of those posh gentleman's clubs – some place like that. But how mistaken can you be? He made his leisurely way across to where *I* was standing. Only me.

And during that whole leisurely journey his expression didn't change.

"Ah! You must be Semple – the great and glorious Semple! I'm Scolopendrid. Greetings, my dear fellow! Our meeting is hugely overdue!"

When I shook his hand I was surprised by how slippery it felt. Which was a shame, because I'd decided I ought to give him a good firm handshake and speak to him like a tried-and-tested equal. In no way like a trespasser.

"Oh, Mr Scolopendrid, you wouldn't *believe* some of the things that have been happening here tonight! Right here in this department!"

"Ah, my dear chap – astonishing – you took the very words straight from my mouth! It's been a nightmare, hasn't it? Pure and utter hell!"

He sniffed the carnation in his buttonhole. Gave a shrug of helpless and bewildered disillusion.

83

"Oh, what *does* take hold of this silly, mad old world on Christmas Eve? I was so much hoping, Mr Simple – Semple – you'd be able to shed a little light on that."

And he continued to gaze at me in anguish, a kind of brotherly anguish, as though he could no longer maintain his boldly smiling front; no longer be stoical about the ordeal we had just passed through, we brave but shaken comrades; exhausted soldiers propping one another up during our stumble from the battleground. As though he could no longer pretend to give a hoot for straightened ties, arched eyebrows or sweetly scented buttonholes.

"You know what we both need, Semple? We need a small restorative."

"Oh, yes," I said, "I'd give anything...!"

But then I broke off.

"I mean – well – no, sir. Not for me."

He didn't seem to hear.

"In fact," he chuckled, "don't you still have a little something tucked away beneath that counter over there?" (Good grief! Had it been mentioned on the *News At Ten*?)

And as a postscript to this question he surprisingly stretched out a sinuous and skinny arm: sent it coiling around corners and slithering over obstacles and winding into dark recesses: until it returned to us like the gliding head of a pinstriped snake, with the bulge of an undigested bottle lodging in its charcoaled throat.

Of course, this couldn't have been the way it *really* was; only the way that it appeared. We must have been closer to the counter than I'd thought.

"Just call me Maurice," he laughed. "Maurice the Magical! The kiddies all love me! Available for weddings, wakes, anniversaries, birthday parties, Halloween – have rabbit, will travel!"

And from first up one sleeve, then up the other, he further produced...no, not a pair of rabbits, but a pair of crystal tumblers.

Then went back to what he had been saying.

"Yes, I can easily imagine that after a very long day – and

especially after all those crazy shenanigans we've just been witnessing – well, a little liquid refreshment would probably be welcome."

"No, I'd better not, sir."

He grinned and gave me a broad wink.

"Of course it might be slightly different if you'd been managing to sleep a little better during your short stay here. Hagalaz & Son may be a lot of things, yet five-star hotel it is *not*! Even I will admit to that!"

"But...er..." I may have stammered a bit. "How did you find out, sir? I mean, when did you first become aware...?"

"Oh, word gets around, you know. Word gets around. Little birds and so forth." He was enjoyably cracking all his finger joints.

By 'so forth', I supposed, he must have meant Hugin and Mugin. Or possibly Muscle Mick. But *little* birds? I scarcely felt surprise when – pat – there came a couple of shrilly indignant squawks.

"Then you don't mind?" I asked.

"Mind? My dear sweet man. What sort of ogre can you conceivably mistake me for?"

For the moment he appeared to have finished with his knuckles. Now, as he spoke, he examined his cufflinks.

"But next year, of course, there'll have to be some changes made. You must come to Hagalaz Hall each night (for be it ever so humble there's no place like home!), come to partake of – I think I can promise you – a not *wholly* inedible meal served with a not *wholly* unquaffable wine; to luxuriate in a steaming hot bath and recline in a well-sprung bed; to enjoy a couple of home-baked biscuits with your early-morning cup of tea; to have a valet lay out your clothes and shine your shoes. Yes, my good sir! How does all of that strike you?"

Well, definitely not like the average offer of your typical meanypants employer. Bosses can be greatly maligned by their staff – even by the very nicest of their staff. He inquired if I'd received my wages.

"I hope you've got the money somewhere good and safe? In your overcoat pocket, perhaps? Which one, old chap?"

So there, you see! Obviously no detail too small to be of interest. Not when there's a caring heart positioned at the helm.

"Well, then, Dick. Let me pour us both a wee dram."

"No, thank you, sir," I repeated. "I'd like to but I'd better not. It really isn't good for me."

And I feel very few could ever fully appreciate the effort which *that* took!

"Ha, ha! Always the wag, always the wag! How you do slay me, Dick, with your priceless sense of humour!"

"But I wasn't joking, sir! I really have to give up on the booze. For the moment, anyhow. I mustn't keep putting it off."

He had suddenly seen how serious I was – and so grew equally serious himself.

"Well, Semple, it's funny you should say that. Because although I think your decision is immensely laudable – and naturally I'll do everything within my power to make you stick to it – I can't help wondering if this is *absolutely* the right moment to make a start."

And to illustrate his point he now looked about him with an air that seemed not merely uneasy but positively fearful.

"I mean...what with all these tiresome powers of darkness bent on playing such silly buggers – and right on our very own doorstep, too! It's even difficult to talk of them, because I don't want you finding out how truly horrible they are, or thinking about the nameless terrors which could be creeping up on us, even as we speak."

"That's very good of you, sir. But, all the same, I really mustn't weaken."

At first he stared at me in silent admiration. After that, he found he simply couldn't stay quiet.

"Ah...even against such odds? I'll no longer try to dissuade you then. So unmistakably the hero!"

He gave a sigh.

"Whereas I myself, I don't possess such fortitude; weakly, I shall have to fall back on…. Oh, my friend, I'm so ashamed. So terrified. So ready to jump ship."

And he frenziedly unscrewed the cap of the whisky bottle. Yet, a fraction unexpectedly, found a moment in which to devote himself to lyricism.

"Though listen, if you will, to its splashings in the glass, its merry glug and gurgle. Savour its many golden lights…that gorgeous amber glow. How warm, how smooth, how comforting!" He was plainly getting a little carried away. "Oh, *Richard*...!" He smacked his lips in keen anticipation.

But suddenly he got sidetracked. He'd noticed something which must have been lying on the floor. And now his arm unwound and speedily slipped off upon some further act of forage.

"Ah, Dick, what's this? Your bracelet! Why, my goodness! I didn't know you'd lost your lovely bracelet."

"Oh, no, Mr Scolopendrid, I didn't! It isn't mine! It really isn't mine!"

And I felt such quantities of panic as I swiftly backed away.

"Well, of course it isn't. Why ever did I think it was? Ah, foolish, foolish me! How humbly I apologize!"

His tone changed.

"Oh gracious – quick – what the – what are they doing to Blitzen?"

I spun round.

He seized my hand.

And within an instant – whether by manic force or magic formula – the manacle was back in place.

He adjusted his tie again; savouringly smoothed back his nutbrown hair; gave me an almost tender smile.

"So even if it wasn't yours, dear Richard...? Well, it seems to me, you haven't had a lot of luck; I'm sure that by now you must deserve some! And finders keepers...right?" He gave a thoughtful little nod.

A despairing moan broke out of me. "But you were the one who found it," I objected.

"Gosh. So I was. And somehow you don't sound too awfully pleased about it," he observed, in a mildly puzzled kind of way.

"Oh, help!" I cried. And then again, but even more forlornly, "Oh, won't somebody help me?"

"Why, of course somebody will! *I* will! Oh, most certainly I'll help you!"

It sounded like he was imitating me trying to comfort Lord Odin on the morning when this whole affair had started.

"What's the matter, Dickie dearest? Is it a fraction tight or something? Tell me, what can I do? You know there's nothing like a drop of fine spirit to take away the pain."

Well, what difference could it make now, I thought. What possible difference? Once that awful ache had begun to reassert itself...

"But just a very little," I mumbled, hopelessly.

"Yes, just a *very* little," he agreed, "and only as a *truly* last resort. For after all, old man, didn't I say I'd do everything within my power to aid you in your recent remarkable resolution...?"

And to show how sincerely he meant this he now struggled to free me of the bracelet.

Yet for all his grunts of effort and persistence; for all his protestations of undying sympathy and unwavering support; for all his bitter railing against fate (on my behalf, of course, not his)...still...there was absolutely nothing for it, he finally admitted, but to accept defeat and to concede the sad alternative: the bracelet would simply have to stay. And for pain relief I'd simply have to drink the whisky. He shook his head and heaved another sigh; then filled my tumbler to the brim.

# 24

At first I took only the most reluctant sip. But then – feeling less hesitant – I allowed myself a second.

Very soon the sips had turned to gulps.

My misery lost much of its acuteness.

"You see, Semple, I was right, wasn't I? Alcohol *does* dull the pain!" He thoughtfully refilled the glass. "So would you like to have some other useful tips while perhaps you're in a mood to learn? Catch up a little on your education?"

But he didn't wait to hear my answer. He flashed me a smile and stretched his arms above his head. He seemed to imply I'd know exactly what he was up to and – what's more – approve of it.

He resumed his normal stance after about a minute. When he did so he was holding something spherical; had produced it from only heaven knew where, like the spare-time magician he prided himself on being. Something spherical and translucent.

He held it out to me.

"I freely confess that I myself tell lies," he said, "play games. An essential ingredient of my artistry. But a crystal ball on the other hand, *this* crystal ball, is constitutionally incapable of holding back the truth. So – come, my friend – gaze into it! See all those happy things which might have been."

*Which might have been?*

"For instance, now…you see those blue skies and those sunlit waters which lie along that other path? Those gatherings, those festivities, those indications of great comfort and delight?" (He was almost carol-singing; perhaps encouraging the young choristers who dimly lined the walls and held aloft their lanterns.) "You know what all of these so accurately foretell? Why, the finding of love and fulfilment, happiness and friendship – respect, tranquillity, good cheer! Oh, my! If you had only played your cards a little more correctly!"

But then he tried to console me.

"You see, for one brief instant in time, you were the man who knew too much! Indisputably…the man of the moment! The man who might have called the shots. For one brief instant in time you were the man who might have won himself a place in history… King Alfred and the cakes, Robert Bruce and the spider, Richard Semple and the Christmas Killjoys! Isn't that thought-provoking?"

And he laughed in commiseration.

"Yet as it is…? That splendid life you glimpse inside this ball? Nothing but the life you'll always know you *could* have had – the one you're going to pine for – yes, achingly and unavailingly and forever." And this time when he cracked his

89

knuckles he did so rather thoughtfully, as though he might have expected them to add their own small, staccato comment.

"Oh, no," I said. "Oh, no."

"It *is* unfortunate. Yet never mind. There's *one* compensation: that if you ever leave this lovely place, at least you'll have your crystal ball. A memorable parting gift. Impossible not to take with you; not to take with you *everywhere*! Impossible to break; impossible not to look into, at least a hundred times, each lonely night and day. Such misery. It's most affecting."

"Oh, no, please don't. No more," I begged.

For not only, in this way, had I been provided with my own ball and chain – not *so* dissimilar to that poor old convict's, although mine was relatively weightless, and apparently invisible to everybody except me – but, almost of more immediate concern, Mr Scolopendrid's whole attitude had changed. He was no longer offering me sympathy.

What he *was* offering was ridicule. Ridicule, coupled with imitation. "*Oh, no! Please don't! No more!* You utter wimp," he said.

I looked down.

"But I guessed as much, you know, the moment I set eyes on you. No guts, I told myself; we'll break him in a jiffy. Rather a disappointment, frankly. I'd have preferred someone I had to pit my wits against; someone worthier of my own unbendable steel! Why, I expect you'll even start to snivel before long. Wimps invariably do. It's tautological." He snapped his fingers at me; snapped them as proficiently as Odin or as Bill. "What are you, Semple? I want you to repeat."

I hesitated. I wasn't sure what he wanted. "A wimp?"

"What sort of wimp?"

"Snivelling?"

"Yes! Correct on both counts. Well, you may not be any kind of a sporting challenge, yet at least you're ready – being so wimplike – to soak up my instructions. Well?"

"Soak up your instructions well."

"Yes. Useless at punctuation but otherwise quite promising." He began to crack his knuckles – lingeringly and pleasurably. "And let's be fair about it. Apart from tonight you've been everything Lord Odin hoped you might be. You've been impatient, disagreeable, smelly. You've spat, you've chewed gum, you've held out your hand and asked for tips. You've scratched yourself like a mangy dog, you've sneezed like a sprinkler system. In short – you've been pretty close to perfection. And even tonight's little lapse (or put it another way: whopping great betrayal) mayn't have been *completely* wasted. It should at least have supplied the enemy with false hope."

He inspected his fingernails. First on one hand, then the other. He seemed satisfied with what he saw.

"No, it could hardly have worked out better, in fact – none of it. It's a pity, perhaps, that you're not to be trusted; but then I suspect you never were. Always just a snivelling wimp..." He raised one lovingly tended eyebrow; looked at me in expectation.

"Just a snivelling wimp," I was forced to agree.

"What a rapscallion I am! What a toe rag!"

"What a rapscallion you are! What a toe rag!"

"No. Not me, *idiot*! You!"

"*Idiot*! You!"

"Oh, you blithering...!"

And he again reached up his arms to heaven but this time purely in exasperation; I sensed that, when he lowered them, there'd be no second crystal ball.

"I must be patient!" he declared. "Long-suffering! Philosophical! I must try to remain my usual cool, calm and thoroughly charming self!"

Then he stopped speaking to the ceiling and addressed his words once more to me.

"So here, you nitwit, are the commandments for next year, which I've been instructed to hand down to you." At this point there followed a queer little giggle – a queer little giggle that launched a flotilla of icy vessels into my bloodstream. "I mean, always supposing that, in your case, there's actually going to *be* a next year."

"Always supposing that in my case...," I gave a gulp, "...there's actually going to *be* a next year..."

"Yes. Well, then. For purposes of simplicity, we'll speak as though there *will* be. So from next Christmas, Semple, you can forget about those things which you've been doing up till now. From next Christmas – and I know this is going to seem altogether *foreign* to your nature – you should even make the odd attempt to wash. And yes, equally out of character, you should even start to smile. Know that word, do you…ever been familiar with it…*smile*? Because from now on, you see, you're solely out to ingratiate yourself with all those little brats and to work hard at winning their complete confidence."

"Winning their complete confidence..."

"But then, as soon as you've got it, here's what you're going to do. You'll whisper in their brattish little ears that you aren't the real Santa. Tell them the real Santa is a vicious old man who absolutely hates children and likes nothing better than to play vile tricks on them. Go on to mention he's become really firm friends with the devil; that the devil has wholly changed Santa; and that the kind of child these two abominate the most is the little goody-two-shoes who's always doing his best to please. Tell them to spread that message far and wide: at school, at kindergarten and in the playgroup: but only – always – to children younger than themselves."

I dutifully repeated the last short phrase.

"And here's something so vital I'll expect you to say it back to me word for word, every syllable. If the brats pass on to any grown-up even one brief whisper of what you've told them…then their details will go straight to the Christmas Bogeyman. Or to use his full and proper title...the Christmas Bogeyman Chameleon."

He seemed to linger over what he said. His eyes lit up with pleasure, as though reflecting a riot of dancing candles on a scrumptious-looking cake.

"Now repeat."

"Repeat. 'If you pass on to any grown-up even one brief whisper of what I've told you – '"

"Yes, yes. All right. I can see you're very clever and that you've absolutely got it. Now then, Semple, to acquaint you further with the talents of the CBC…to make known to you its sheer range and versatility..."

He paused a moment, in quiet appreciation.

"Sheer range and versatility," I said. He told me to shut up.

"Flying lizard, leaping toad, bloodsucking tarantula…," he enumerated. (Ticking off these items on his skinny – rubbery – maybe treble-jointed fingers.) "He can assume the form of anything he likes. It will be your own delightful duty to worm out of whichever brat is currently beside you exactly what might frighten him the most. When you've successfully established *that*, you will describe how – oh, dear! – this specific type of beast is the very one which conceals itself beneath all children's beds or duvets, lurks in wardrobes, toy cupboards or dolls' houses. It may spring out at any moment of the morning, afternoon or evening – but usually, like Dracula, prefers to wait until dark. (Has no problem whatever over light bulbs – can instantly cause them to explode, purely by looking at them.) You will go on to explain how it can drop down…*plop*!…*right in the middle of your pretty little face, my sweet child, if you've managed at last to cry yourself to sleep, or of your pale and terrified little face, dear precious, if you haven't. With its dribbling mouth and bloodshot eyes and suppurating sores, it will at that point, very slowly, commence to put out all its feelers…* And so on – and so on – bla bla bla! Well, anyway, Semple, I'm sure by now you get the picture. Just don't let them think it's pleasant."

"Think it's pleasant."

But for the second time Scolopendrid snapped his fingers. "All right. All right. No more of these imbecilic repetitions. They've grown as tedious as you have."

He studied my face.

"And do you know something? If I didn't believe the Master wholly incapable of error, I'm still not sure that I myself would ever want to bother with you. Not even as a calculated risk. You mustn't take offence."

Again I looked down at the floor; having no good idea of how I should respond.

"So Semple. Dispel my doubts, if you can. Ask me a question."

"What?"

"An intelligent question."

"Ask you a question?"

"And still he repeats! He just repeats. Yes, you parrot! An intelligent and penetrating question. To demonstrate that you've absorbed, and pondered, and have finally – could this be conceivable? – finally seen the light! Seen the light...changed sides! Yes," he nodded, "in theory at least, I suppose that needn't be impossible. I should at any rate *attempt* to keep an open mind."

He winked at me again, with the scepticism in his tone matched only by the blatant cat-and-mouse amusement in his eyes.

"Well, Semple? Can there be something that's detaining you? I haven't got all day, you know."

# 25

It's always hard when people invite you to put an intelligent question. Your brain seems to seize up.

On the children's homecoming every afternoon, Harriet would invariably say to them: "What have you asked in school today?" We'd thought it might encourage the development of good inquiring minds.

And I remember one particular winter's afternoon – when a migraine had prevented me from going off to manage the bank as I usually did – I remember Peter's thoughtfully answering, through a mouthful of cake or something, "Not very much...not that I can think of."

But then he'd gone on, "Though, as it happens, I've got an interesting question right now. It's one for you, Dad."

"Okay."

"Why are you standing here in the kitchen when you should be upstairs working on the story? We've been waiting for it for *ages* – haven't we, Nao?"

Mmm. Perhaps I'd been misguided ever to mention I was writing them a book. But I'd thought that if I really gritted my

94

teeth and went ahead and *told* them about it...then this time I might stand a better chance of actually getting it done.

And now – despite feeling fairly apprehensive – I was looking forward to hearing the verdict of the two readers it was principally meant for.

But I never did.

The climax still needed polishing. The climax in Hyde Park: police and soldiers closing in on Tanner with orders to shoot him on sight. And Johnny having to be whisked off home and learn that his adventures in Elm had actually been real – not merely the effects of illness.

So – like my three main characters, who had each started off by losing something – I had lost things, too. And one of those had been the will to continue working on my story.

Along, in fact, with the loss of practically everything else. Including, all these years later, the all-but-completed manuscript...so close to the spot where poor Tanner, in the interests of the public safety, had nearly had to die.

Of course, Johnny and Amelia – and even Tanner and Miss Cellaneous – had finally got things back.

And, similarly, I myself – after hearing tonight about my family – I as well could imagine recovering bits and pieces which I'd never thought *would* be recoverable.

For instance...the will to write.

The will.

But would I ever get the opportunity?

# 26

"There's only one question I'd like answered. But why would you bother? I'm a nobody."

"Well, that – most certainly – we can agree on. Yet even so. You make it sound intriguing."

"Worse, I'm a nobody you don't trust. So however *intriguing* my question...or however sensible my ideas..."

"You have ideas?" he inquired, eagerly.

"I might have." The shrug I gave was intended to appear casual.

"Now then, Semple, you mustn't start jumping to conclusions. Depending on what he may contribute, even a nobody can occasionally turn out to be a *some*body. A somebody, admittedly, of very minimal importance. But I think it *has* happened. So long ago, I confess, that it's become wholly buried in the mists of time – and, indeed, may only be apocryphal."

"Once in the blue moon?" I asked him, nervously.

"Yes, I think we might be allowed to stretch a point here. To exaggerate a bit. To humour you a little and say once in the blue moon."

Did I detect the merest hint of a shift in attitude?

"All right, then," I said. "Of course, I don't pretend to be anything out of the ordinary but I do feel that at rare moments I could possibly come up with a pleasantly nasty idea."

I hesitated.

"For instance, you haven't yet mentioned the possibility of my picking a few pockets while the brats are sitting beside me in the sleigh. Often little boys will carry about with them some of their most highly prized possessions."

"Oh – excellent, excellent! I would only quarrel with your slightly odd choice of adjective: why just a *few*? And also...can it, I wonder, be absolutely squared with our need to gain the creatures' confidence? (Oh, but why not, why not?) So that's definitely one suggestion I feel I should take note of."

Yet unexpectedly he wheeled about and waved a rubbery finger in the direction of the castle.

"Hugin! Mugin! Don't you dare inform the Master. *I* want to be the one who'll see that sudden happy gleam irradiate his eye."

On hearing this, there was nothing for me to do but let out a real whinge. "You're going to pretend that it was *you* who thought of it! Aren't you?"

"Oh, again, old chap, I find myself in absolute agreement. You're so utterly on the ball! Yet answer me this: supposing our positions were reversed: would you yourself do any different?"

"No. To be honest, I don't suppose I should..." Grudgingly

fair-minded. "But now I shan't tell you my other idea."

"And what's that?"

"Well, to tear the little girls' dresses. Or else have a phial of ink constantly on hand. Because – for a meeting with Santa – won't they all be wearing their very favourite things?"

"They'd better be!" he declared. "Otherwise we'd look upon it as an insult."

"Then only picture the hours of subsequent distress. And – equally – won't their mothers be furious! But would it ever occur to mothers to lay the blame on *us*? No, I really don't think so. Oh, drat it!" I exclaimed.

I stamped my foot in frustration.

"Why, whatever's the matter?" asked Mr Scolopendrid. Again, with the very liveliest of interest.

"I've just realized how you tricked me. Oh, drat! *I* could have told the Master. *I* could have seen that sudden happy gleam irradiate his eye."

"Yes, you did rather fall for it, didn't you? I'm so terribly sorry! What more can I say?"

"Well, I suppose you're just too clever for me. That's the truth of it."

"Yes, I suppose I am, really. But don't let it depress you. Actually, I'm just too clever for most people. But I knew, of course – knew from the first moment I set eyes on you – what a rare and wonderful acquisition you'd soon turn out to be. Now, what was your question, my good fellow: the one you felt too shy and insignificant to ask?"

"And also," I reminded him, "too scared about seeming presumptuous."

"Exactly right. And also too scared about seeming presumptuous."

"Although, in fact, it wasn't only *those* things which were holding me back."

"No? There was something *else*? Something other than your insignificance, shyness and presumption? Good gracious! Tell me what!"

But first I glanced around the department: left, right – up, down, in front of me, behind. I didn't mind his noticing my hesitation.

"Because the trouble is...have they told you of that busybody sent here earlier by STARS?"

Mr Scolopendrid nodded, gravely.

"Well, in fact I was only half-listening," I said, "but I seem to remember he was boasting about their bugging, and their CCTV, and goodness knows what else – really, I was just *so* bored! But what I mean is, sir...well, supposing that, out of the sheer goodness of your heart, you were ever to humour a complete nobody like me, by deigning to answer some stupid little question which he'd – oh, quite unbelievably! – had the effrontery to put to you? Wouldn't it obviously spoil everything, *everything*, if they truly had the power to listen in? Oh!" – and suddenly I spluttered – "what gall, what cheek, what brazen impudence! To think that they can stoop so low as to spy on us...yes, actually to spy on us!"

I shook my head furiously but couldn't find the words fully to express my contempt.

My companion, however, didn't require words.

He executed a handspring.

"And would you believe it, Semple? Up until now I was honestly convinced that you were one of them!" He said this laughingly, after he had let me enthuse for a while over his being so wonderfully acrobatic. "Have another drink," he added.

This time I raised no objection. My throat was dry. I needed lubrication.

In fact, he had to upend the bottle and even shake it. Yet, fortunately, I got close to half a glassful.

"But I *was* one of them! Until things changed. After all, sir, I hadn't yet met *you*. And I let myself be taken for a complete ride."

"Yet all the same," he said, "I feel I may have underestimated you."

"What – me, Mr Shcolopendrid? You must be joking!"

"Still. I suppose in a way you underestimated me, as well."

I didn't quite follow.

"You were talking about bugs and CCTV," he said. "Remember? But of course that was the first thing I attended to – just now, before I left the castle."

"Oh, sir, I'm such a befuddled old fool... What was?" Although I *had* raised my glass again, I very swiftly lowered it. I wanted him to know how utterly intent I was on trying to clear my head.

"Why, my good friend, the temporary destruction of all their technological equipment – naturally."

"Ah, yes, of course! I see. Naturally! But why only temporary?" I had difficulty, too, with 'temporary'. He didn't seem to mind.

"Because, confound 'em, they always appear to keep one step ahead. They'll have it all repaired again by morning."

"Yet not *before* the morning?" And I hoped that from my tone he could discern the full extent of my relief. "You're sure that right now we're safe? Absolutely safe?"

"Dick, I'm so glad to discover you're a cautious man: something else that'll qualify you for a top post on our executive. But at the same time you must learn to trust my talent for destruction; that's all I'd like to say! Now, then? What's your question?"

"Well, also about destruction. Which is undoubtedly coincidental! But not just temporary," I said, speaking carefully, because the effect of all that drink could easily have been a far worse slurring of my words. "This is about...this is about... well, this is about more *permanent* destruction."

"Promising, promising. Nothing ever quite so interesting, in my view."

I felt sufficiently encouraged; I took a breath in preparation.

"Mr Shcolopendrid, is there any way – oh please, please tell me that there isn't! – is there any way in which...in which we ourselves could ever be destroyed?"

Again, he was delighted.

"Well, do you know, my friend...I am impressed! I'm always on the lookout for intelligent questions, as I suspect you may have realized by now. But I seldom meet up with one that's so all-round intelligent as that! And even you yourself, incredibly, referred to it as stupid! Oh, fie! You shouldn't be like me, you know, hiding your megawatt light beneath a bushel."

He pumped my hand; he slapped me on the shoulder. (Retreated a little and – with obvious absentmindedness – wiped his palms upon his handkerchief.)

"But no, Dick, you shouldn't be alarmed. There's only one way in which we could ever *permanently* be destroyed; and that's never going to happen, never in a thousand years. Never in a million."

"You're certain?" And the depth of my concern must still have been glaringly apparent.

"Well, how do you suppose anyone's ever going to guess the wording? *Anyone*, let alone a bunch of poxy, ragamuffin kids!"

"Kids?"

"Yes. Even the proper wording couldn't bring us down, except from the mouths of loathsome, interfering guttersnipes." Again, I had a hunch he just meant ordinary children. "I admit it would take only about a hundred of them…or maybe only fifty…but they'd all have to be together in one place and to say the words in unison – and how do you think *that* could ever happen? Forget the organizational nightmare; the brats would also need to know the spell. Obviously they would. So now, Dick, I ask you! Don't you feel I've said enough to set your mind at ease?"

"Thank you," I replied, in heartfelt tones. "You have."

"For instance, would it ever occur to *you* to cry out: 'By the stars, in the lie –'?" He was hit by a jet-propelled wasp.

Well, that's what it seemed like. Even the drunkest man on earth might have turned cold dead sober with the shock.

Whoosh!

Pow!

Zing!

This creature (this *creature*? this projectile!) had come zooming at him out of nowhere. Had dived about his neck – and nose and ears and eyes – much faster than anyone's astonished gaze could ever follow it. It recalled to me the terrifying CBC.

However, I soon realized that it wasn't a hornet or a bee – although, clearly, a large insect of some variety, possibly South

American. It was about the size and shape of a sugared almond but I formed the impression it was softer than a sugared almond. I thought it looked like a jujube – or a pastille – or something even spongier and more jellylike. Except that neither jujubes nor pastilles nor sugared almonds were ever sufficiently bright, or sufficiently piercing, or sufficiently blue.

In any case, Scolopendrid had hurled himself sideways in an effort to avoid it. Had beaten at it frantically. Had tried to bat it off like the angry wasp it very plainly wasn't.

But then instinct had given place to intellect and he had actually managed to submit – as if suddenly remembering what people said about not running away from enraged animals...did the same apply to insects? He even stood to attention and kept his eyes open. I felt respect for him; or *would* have felt respect for him, if I'd stayed calm enough to feel respect for anyone.

The onslaught ended. The thing whizzed off. Back into nowhere. There ensued a long and pregnant pause, before either of us spoke. "What *was* that?" I asked.

Scolopendrid, too, was pallid and sweaty and shaken. Well, naturally, naturally! In his place I should probably have gone berserk.

But despite this...he was *smiling*!

And that wasn't natural – wasn't natural in the slightest – even if his smile was a little closer to a death's-head grin than to a casual nod accompanying some comment on the weather.

"What was what?" he said.

I stared at him. He stared straight back. At least one of us, I thought, must now have lost his marbles.

"Because if you're under the impression you may have noticed something," he observed – with his voice, by this time, having more or less returned to normal – "I think, Dick, you're probably a little on edge and overexcited. For here, tonight, it's only too easy, isn't it, to start imagining things? Oh, my, yes! Mmm. Now, what were we discussing?"

# 27

It was hard to disguise my feeling of unease about what had taken place. And this plainly worried him. I don't know what line of logic he was following but he chose to ascribe my reaction – I should have thought my only-too-understandable reaction – to the fact that I must be losing faith in him; in him and Lord Odin and in everything they stood for.

I denied it vehemently, of course. Yet now the notion had occurred to him, the question mark remained.

"Here! Let me convince you!" I cried.

"But how, Dick – how?" So much wanting reassurance.

I hesitated. "I have another idea which I feel may be of interest."

"Ah...?"

"But please – this time – you mustn't let Lord Odin think that it was yours."

I saw the question mark begin to disappear.

"Good gracious...as if I *would*! Oh, never – never! You can trust me, Dick. Don't you realize how fully you can trust me?"

"Hmm. Well no, sir, I'm not so sure. You're just a little on the crafty side."

"Oh, my dear fellow. How can you possibly believe that? Why, good gracious. Cross my heart and hope to die!" He was clearly rather pleased.

So I allowed myself to be persuaded. I gave a sigh and a still slightly dubious look, but then launched almost proudly into this glorious new design of mine.

"Now just try to imagine, Mr Scolopendrid – "

"Oh, Maurice, please."

He pronounced it with a French accent.

"Well, then, Maureece – oh, what an honour, are you sure? – I want you to imagine this. We're on the air again...though (ha, ha) we don't realize it, we think their bugs are still defective. In fact, we so much don't realize it (ha, ha!) that you say you're going to tell me all about that magic and almighty spell, the one which potentially – *potentially*! – could destroy everything Lord Odin

102

and his doting band of followers have always worked for. You say you've at last decided to let me into that precious, powerful and most tantalizing secret."

"I do?" he asked, with some faint air of reservation.

"But now switch to their end: to their operations room. *What*? *Can this possibly be true*? *Is it just being handed to us on a plate*? *Have we really got them, then, at last*? They daren't quite believe their luck, you see, but hopes rise high and hearts climb into mouths. The tension mounts. Excitement reaches fever pitch. Soon becomes unbearable. You give another twist to the screw. Still yet a further one. Until...well, finally...*finally*...you'll bend and whisper in my ear."

"What will I whisper?"

"I imagined you'd actually whisper the secret – is it some form of runic text? – whilst making very sure, of course, that your hand's in front of your mouth! We wouldn't want to encourage any over-optimistic lip-readers!"

"No," he agreed. Yet he spoke more quietly than I might have expected. His reaction reminded me a little of Bill's after I had got the bracelet off – but hadn't known how soon I would be stuck with it again!

"So, Maurice? What do you think? Oh, the disappointment and the broken dreams! The nervous breakdowns! Resignations. Suicides."

Scolopendrid rubbed his hands together. "Oh, yes, I like the notion of *that*. I do quite like the notion of *that*." Why should I sense, then, that he still had reservations?

"I rather hoped you might."

"But unfortunately, you know, it simply won't do."

"It won't?"

"Because you seem to have forgotten something. While you'd so easily be able to prevent them from reading your lips, you wouldn't at all be able to prevent them from reading your thoughts. Which tends to make your scheme just the tiniest bit flawed...I think you'd possibly agree?"

It was true: I had forgotten their ability to read my thoughts.

"Or possibly you wouldn't?" said Mr Scolopendrid. Reflectively.

"Wouldn't what, sir?"

"Agree about your scheme being flawed." And he continued to regard me with an air of deep suspicion. "After all, the essence of the plan was only that I should whisper something. It didn't have to be the secret, did it? But isn't it surprising that you didn't think to point this out?"

"Surprising? No, not at all, sir. I said 'I imagined you'd whisper the secret' but in the end I wouldn't actually have allowed you to do so – I hadn't forgotten they can read my mind!" I said this quite reproachfully. "Really, I would have thought that was *totally* understood between us! But... Well, you see... What with all the whisky you've been giving me..."

"Why, yes, of course! Of course! How could I have overlooked that? How could I not have made allowances? So terribly insensitive!"

I wasn't sure if he was serious or not but I hoped – and decided to assume – he was. I said: "And so there's nothing to stop us right now, is there, Maurice, from carrying on with my idea...?" I knew this sounded pretty lame.

"Except, Dick, that we're *not* on the air right now...as you so quaintly put it." His tone was sweetly patient but I realized that I was sinking in his estimation. Just had to be.

Though I felt marginally reassured by his subsequent comment.

"It provided a pleasant little interlude, however. A pipe dream. An ever-welcome touch of frivolity. I'm sure we all need a touch of frivolity at times, to help us remain cheery." He paused, then cracked his knuckles – cheerily – and remarked with a laugh, "And now, of course, I know the content of your *next* intelligent question."

I thought this was very clever of him, especially considering that *I* didn't. Besides... Hadn't he led me to assume that only one would be required?

"Oh, bother!" I complained. "Oh, bother! How you do keep on forestalling me!"

He preened himself. Again, it was as if I couldn't have said anything more flattering.

"Well, isn't it obvious?" he continued. "Once their spying system's been restored, what's to prevent them from finding out the secret anyway? *That's* what you're wanting to ask."

Was it? If so, the question would have been so *very* intelligent that even I, the questioner, wouldn't have understood its meaning.

"Because, Dick, let's face it, I'm afraid you're only human. When you know you simply mustn't think a thing, no power on earth can ever stop you thinking it. Right?"

And as he'd done before, he adopted a sweetly pitying and sympathetic smile. I was appalled.

"But I don't know the secret, sir! How could I possibly know the secret? You were interrupted! Something interrupted you! Don't tell me you've forgotten?"

"Yes, in all honesty, I have. But why should that matter? If *you* remember it…that's good enough for me."

My panic receded, somewhat.

"If you say I was interrupted, then I'm very sure I was," he further confirmed.

"Just a second or two after you had started." I needed to make this very clear.

"Indeed – as you suggest – just a second or two after I had started."

But for some reason my panic stopped receding. It looked round at me and re-approached.

"And a second or two would equal…what?" he asked. "Shall we say…as many as three short words a second…?" He ruminated. "Which means, of course, you'll still have heard – at the very worst – only about six of them. Neither here nor there, you might think. Yet, on the *other* hand… Well, as it happens, there are merely a dozen words in the whole caboodle! Oh dear. What another fine mess we seem to have got ourselves into!"

"But I didn't hear them! I didn't! Not any of them!" My brain was beating about like a trapped bird under a low ceiling. "Besides. Don't forget. I'll be away from here before their system's been repaired! *Long* before it's been repaired!"

"Yet, Dick, I thought you spoke about returning here next year?"

"Well, yes...but not if it won't suit you. No, of course not! Not if it won't suit you, Mr Scolopendrid."

"Maurice."

"Maurice."

"Oh my, though. What a puzzlement! And frankly, then, you seem to see yourself as being expendable? Am I right?"

I wasn't quite sure how to answer that.

Yet, suddenly – and mercifully – I thought I might have found a valid argument. One that was really about to win my case for me. "But, come to that, Maurice, what's to prevent them from reading *your* thoughts?"

My hopes were disappointed.

"Simple," he said. "They've never had access. But you at some point...tragically, *you* must have negotiated. Well – in fact – we know that you negotiated. Don't we?"

But, instinctively, I still struggled to build up my defences. With blind desperation now, rather than valid argument.

"No," I said. "Their man could already read my thoughts. Even before he turned up here tonight."

"Then I don't mean to insult you, Dick, but at some time in the past you must have supplied him with the key...probably through showing some kind of soppy sentimental weakness which he took to be a strength."

Although Maurice didn't mean to insult me, he made at least three of those words sound reasonably insulting.

But soon, as if only wanting my forgiveness, he attempted a different form of approach which, as before, was certainly a little more encouraging. Initially.

"Yet why are we so glum, old chap? It's true I've committed a misdemeanour. But good, you know, can frequently come out of bad." He grinned; and without apparent motivation, began to limber up his fingers, as though they weren't already quite limber enough. "Oh, yes. Good can so often come of bad, I swear it."

"In this case," I had to ask, "what kind of good are we thinking of, exactly?"

At first he seemed uncertain whether he should tell me.

"All right, then. The good thing is – we happen to have this truly marvellous method of dispelling memory. Enormously effective," he said. "*And* satisfying." He looked down at his hands and gave another grin.

He didn't say for whom it might be satisfying. Even *enormously* satisfying.

"But I've got no memory to dispel! No memory at all! The whisky – lack of sleep – those thousand upsets which we've both been through… Can you be surprised at it, my getting so confused?"

Yet was he even listening? "And all part of the same happy news, Dick: just a short while ago the Master himself arrived here, in person! What a treat! What a privilege!"

I didn't altogether see the connection.

"However," he added, "owing to his preferred means of transportation, he always needs to rest for a while, before – as it were – gathering himself together again. But have no fear. In only a short time he'll be able to bless us in abundance, with his usual gifts of good fellowship, rich experience and charismatic guidance."

"Guidance on what?" I wasn't sure if I wanted to hear the answer.

"Oh, well." Mr Scolopendrid grew vague. "Length of time…amount of pressure…where to apply that pressure. Little things. Nothing too major."

He laughed – all vagueness disappeared.

"But I know! To give you some idea, why not picture him as standing in the gallery of an operating theatre, inside a teaching hospital: the world-famous surgeon following, with pride, the eager debut of a favourite pupil?"

He looked down modestly; then playfully got the jitters; maybe to demonstrate a favourite pupil's initial panic at being watched.

But, after that, he returned to his finger-flexing; in happy anticipation.

"You know, I'm so *proud* of my hands. Isn't that foolish? Well, I suppose everybody's allowed to be proud of something. I've even met people who were proud of their necks, would you believe? Their *necks*! Extraordinary, isn't it? And people who were proud of their skins." He threw up his hands in astonishment. "How would you say, Dick, that you feel about your own neck? What kind of value would you set upon your own skin?"

He tipped his head to one side and again seemed to be assessing me.

"Of course, I could always have gone ahead without Lord Odin's being here; without his standing in the gallery, so to speak. But naturally I wouldn't want to jump the gun at all. Because although he – "

"Have gone ahead with *what*?"

" – because although he rang me up no more than half an hour ago, told me I might receive a little Christmas present here tonight, he hadn't at that point *irrevocably* decided."

Whilst speaking, Mr Scolopendrid had absent-mindedly turned down the collar of my coat, which I'd put up when Blitzen and I had been away on our travels.

"Sorry," he murmured, after a further moment of appearing to be sizing something up. "Force of habit! At Hagalaz & Son we're always anxious to maintain a very strict dress code."

Reasonable explanation?

And yet, in that case, why should I be growing steadily more uneasy?

"Oh, Mr Shcolopendrid!" I said.

"Maurice!" he corrected me.

"I think I *may* have found another interesting idea."

It was one, indeed, which I'd been feverishly trying to work out during the past few minutes. But its details were still unclear. I didn't see how even its two most basic requirements could be met.

And, anyway, all the danger that would be attached to it…!

So why, then, should I be getting this very strong feeling about it? Almost a sense of being urged on?

"Ah, what a man of ideas you are! How valuable you might have been."

"*Might have been*?"

108

"Did I say that? No, surely not. Though it's true, I always had such trouble with my tenses. French irregular verbs! Latin conjugations! Oh, how you would have laughed at me! My subjunctives – my future conditionals – what a constant fount of entertainment to all my little classmates! Did you, dear Dick...did *you* ever study Latin?"

Yet at this point I wasn't paying much attention; it was only later it was revealed to me what he had said. But still. I suddenly resurfaced to realize some question had been asked and rather than have to say I hadn't been listening I mutely shook my head. I didn't want to annoy him.

He paused.

"So what's this last idea of yours? I'm sorry, my dear fellow, I mean this *latest* idea of yours?"

No, it really didn't bode too well: the fact that something made him believe he should be sensitive about such things.

"Ah, yes," I said. "But if you don't mind, before we go into all of that, I think I must just tootle along to the Gents. I want to be able to concentrate *completely* on each of the exciting details. Also, of course, I want to be able to appreciate in full our dear Master's approaching visit..."

Unfortunately, though, before I could take more than just a few steps, one of his hands had settled on my collar. This time pulling it up, rather than turning it down.

"Oh no, Dick, *no*! Nothing but nerves. As soon as Lord Odin arrives, you'll no longer need the Gents."

And I assumed he must have made some signal, for the two ragged adventurers – those whom I'd last seen marching in line behind the Barbie dolls – were soon making their way towards us, lightly springing over any obstacle which impeded their short cut. And one of these Aussies winked at me. "Now, you don't really intend to hurry off and leave us, cobber? Not when we've just dropped in...all matey, like...to pay you our respects?"

Soon, his partner was shadow-boxing: making vicious lunges which left an imaginary opponent writhing and groaning on the floor. "Oh, kindly stop yer blubbering, sport, 'less you really want me putting the boot in! Tell me, sport, is that what you're after now, what you're really *begging* for, now?" Stout tan

109

leather on the end of sunburnt leg.

"Hey, that's enough now, killer," said the first.

Then added, as he turned back to myself, "Always likes to pretend he's beating up some senior citizen or other. He's a bit...well, you know…" He tapped himself on the temple, whilst giving me another wink. "Doolally."

I said to Scolopendrid:

"Then may I just settle an old score with Blitzen? I'd like to climb up on his back and…and, I don't know…give him a good hard tweak where it's really going to hurt!"

"Ah, Dick. I was hoping your idea was *much* more interesting than that."

"Good gracious! That wasn't it; that wasn't it at all! That was just a sideline!"

"Oh, I'm so relieved! You had me quite worried! So please be a good chap and finally get it off your chest."

I had to swallow. "It really isn't all that far advanced. You see, I was only thinking…that if..."

And then I took the plunge. Decided I simply had to dispense with caution, trust in all those promptings I thought I'd been receiving, make things up as I went along.

"I was only thinking," I said, speaking very slowly, "I was only thinking that if…"

"Semple, you're repeating yourself again!"

"…that if the toys on our side were to rise up and stride into battle against the toys on their side..."

He raised an eyebrow.

"…how our lot could then start to bite and kick and punch. Hit below the belt. Gang up – three onto one, maybe." It was beginning to come more quickly. "So that afterwards..."

"Yes, go on."

"So that afterwards we could get to hurt them in earnest, crush them to a pulp, smash their big stupid heads together, make them really yell out for mercy."

"Which of course," he said, "we wouldn't give?" I felt I might be starting to arouse his interest.

"Not that we'd ever *mean* to commit any fouls," I pointed out, sanctimoniously.

"Mean to commit any fouls?" he cried. "Good heavens, no! What *has* got into you?"

What had got into me, I believed, could conceivably have been described as a grain of confidence. Or even optimism.

"But listen, Maurice, here is the good bit – although obviously it would all, all of it, depend on *you*! Without *your* inspirational presence who could even dream of anything so challenging?" He nodded, agreeably. "Yet nothing is beyond Maurice the Magical! You could even transform this place into a sort of temporary theatre, couldn't you, have dozens of brats sitting out there, thinking that they've only come to see a pantomime and at first hating it as they watch all the weaker toys get injured, watch them suffer, watch them gradually fall apart – yes, at first hating it, all those dozens of brats, screwing up their eyes, pressing their hands against their ears (oh, this will be the very stuff of nightmares, a lifetime of nightmares), most of them screaming out in terror...but growing just a little bit fascinated too, peeping out through increasingly splayed fingers, having the first strong seeds implanted in them of what may later come to be a real thirst for cruelty...?"

"Mmm," he said. "Mmm. Mmm..." And then again: "Mmm..."

What made this easier, of course, I knew that I was playing to a good audience.

"Oh, Maurice, do you think – on returning home from the performance – some of them might immediately start to experiment: pull the stuffing out of teddy bears, smash up china dolls, snap the heads off tin soldiers...?"

I felt that by now I had possibly said enough. Even Muscle Mike the Neanderthal would probably have caught my drift.

"Oh, lovely, lovely," said Scolopendrid. "So beautiful! So very beautiful it almost makes me want to *sing*!"

"Good on you, cobber," said the adventurer – the one who was the more laid-back and communicative. "Right on." But I wasn't sure which of us he was talking to.

"By far the best notion any Santa ever had," continued Mr Scolopendrid. "Oh, what a prince! What a poet! What a paragon!"

111

"What a peach," drawled the other; still, however, looking at Scolopendrid rather than at me.

"And I'd have the power, Dick – oh, yes, indeed I would – the moment that Lord Odin comes: the power to turn this part of Hagalaz & Son into quite the quaintest little bijou theatre in the whole of Britain...and even the power to conjure up an audience full of the most impressionable and tender-hearted little darlings you ever saw, all dewy-eyed with expectation. And, oh, my goodness! Speak of the devil. Here he is."

Whereupon, this modest magician now swept forward to pay homage to his Master, and even before Lord Odin had reached us was executing quite the lowest and most elegant of courtly bows. It was only a pity he hadn't got a feathered hat to doff.

"Here, killer, take a look at *this*!"

"Go away. I'm busy. Got me another senior citizen."

"Your loss, mate. Missing out on something good. *Really* bonzer!"

# 28

"Oh, Maurice, Maurice..."

Lord Odin pronounced it in the English way.

"How people *do* have to pay for your mistakes! Good evening, Mr Semple."

Following his bow, Scolopendrid had chosen to kneel at the feet of his Master. "Then does this mean, Lord," he inquired excitedly, "that you have come to a decision?"

"Decision?"

"My Christmas gift, if you remember...?"

"Oh, yes – that permission you've been craving?" He sighed. "Well, thanks to your own foolishness and your flagrant overstepping of the mark" – he sighed again – "I can't see any acceptable alternative. Can you?"

Yet, despite his sighs and his acerbity, it was almost as if he were speaking to a son: a son who'd been sufficiently chastised, who had borne up well under punishment, and who could now perhaps be pardoned. Paternal indulgence seemed to emanate from every pore. When he used his lit cigar to wave away the two adventurers – and one of them, with careless shrug and openly mock-serious salute, protectively led off the other (still deep into shadow-boxing) – he only smiled, forbearingly. Scolopendrid remained on his knees.

"Oh, most merciful, munificent and bewitching Lord! You bestow such benevolence upon your poor unworthy subjects!" His hands were clasped appreciatively beneath his chin. "And also on myself," he added gratefully.

"That's very true. But in this case, Maurice, you leave me with no option. You've always been something of a loose cannon: in many ways a source of stimulation and of challenge...of breezy entertainment in a frequently quite boring world...but tonight you've been a source of risk. Almost, I might venture…"

"But, Lord, may I suggest – I mean, in a context such as this – not *source*? I myself, I shouldn't go for *source*. Not in these present joyful circumstances!"

Their conversation was not an easy one to follow. Even Lord Odin looked a bit perplexed.

"On the other hand," continued Scolopendrid, with that same innocent yet unashamedly roguish air, "one could always go for 'fons'. The creature understands no Latin. And 'stella', too," he added rakishly; his nose and chin – even his very cheekbones – appearing practically to quiver with pure mischief.

"Ah. Now, of course, I understand your game. You're a child, Maurice. Forever testing. Forever trying to push back boundaries."

But this was approval enough, apparently. Scolopendrid directed me a sidelong glance.

"'Lux'," he smiled. "'Vis'," he grinned. "'Vim - vi - vires'," he chuckled. "That's accusative, ablative and plural thrown in…no extra charge! Goodness! But I must be having a good day!"

I felt quite enormously puzzled.

Apart from anything else…what made him suppose I understood no Latin?

113

"Maurice," said Odin, blowing five utterly perfect smoke rings, "don't you sometimes feel that in spite of all my warnings you occasionally sail a *trifle* close to the wind?"

But his appreciation still showed: though whether of smoke rings or of those daring navigational feats it wasn't altogether clear.

"'Invenio, invenire, inveni, inventum.' 'Utor, uti, usus sum!' Oh, they can call me just an intellectual jackanapes, if they feel so inclined. But who could deny my life-enhancing spirit?"

"Now that's enough! You've had your fun!" The Master's tone had suddenly acquired an edge; had lost its quality of gently amused restraint. "May I suggest that, first of all, you arise from that ridiculous position?"

The life-enhancer scrambled to his feet.

Showed instantaneous remorse.

"I seek forgiveness, Lord. Oh, what a show-off! (I mean me, of course, not you!) Too much excitement before bed – what other excuse would I ever have? None whatsoever...except, maybe, the glory of your gracious presence? My knowledge of your liberality? Anticipation of your generous gift?"

One could possibly see just a *little* of why Lord Odin put up with him.

And, although Scolopendrid now restlessly resumed the flexing of his fingers, he soon stopped and resolutely put his hands behind his back. He must have known how very irritating it could get.

He cast me another glance.

"However, I was about to request, Lord, that you might withhold it for a while. That very generous gift."

"You *were*?" If Mrs Mangosteen had danced before him naked, or Mr Daglock, or Mr Chugglefroth, it seemed Lord Odin could scarcely have experienced more surprise. He even leaned forward a little; for all the world as if he required some repetition.

"A double-edged reward," said Scolopendrid, "for one of the most rib-tickling notions you may well have listened to since lunchtime."

"Semple's?"

114

"Semple's? Oh, yes. I suppose he might have had a hand in it – a *small* hand – to tell the truth I didn't really notice."

"Hmm. Very well, Maurice. Clarify."

Clarification followed. Lord Odin became transfixed. His deep blue eye – beneficent as sunlight falling out of a cloudless sky – came to rest, inscrutably, on me.

"I must admit, Semple, that it has a certain piquancy. A certain...*je ne sais quoi*. And who'd ever say I'm not fair-minded?" ("Not I, not I!" exclaimed his minion – despite, no doubt, having to suppress a broad streak of resentment that *I* was the one now being applauded.) "Here is the co-author of the plot. Of *course* he must be present at the play."

But, after a minute, that almond-shaped and piercing eye did indeed go back to Scolopendrid.

"Truly...an inspired collaboration. As always, Maurice, when you are good, you are very, very good."

Kind words. I saw the chest of the magician swell. He became less cadaverous. Pride bestowed on him a presence. Even his buttonhole began to glow.

And I wasn't simply imagining that. His buttonhole was just a red carnation but it grew brighter by the instant. Steadily brighter. Until it appeared so energized by its very radiance that it abruptly tore away and spiralled to the ceiling.

I had the impression that it simply waited there to pick up its instructions.

And soon there were hundreds of red carnations adorning the white, moon-dappled ceiling.

Yet okay, so what? Party tricks, not proper transformations. Not spells to make your garden grow.

But Maurice the Magical was now muttering to himself and probably oblivious to everything but his enchantment. He had both eyes closed. Odin had one eye very much open.

Then the flowers exploded.

A million crimson sparks and crystals. They made a thousand fountains. They showered down all about us. Formed patterns as they fell.

And somehow I already knew – the characters they made were symbols from an ancient alphabet.

Whereupon, things rapidly became less pretty, more prosaic. No longer floral displays and fireworks; now...export of merchandise, import of furniture. And furnishings. Seats flew in through closed windows – *apparently* closed windows; floated down in tiers; soon composed a dozen rows of well-upholstered stalls.

Boxes, dress circle and upper circle, too. Cherubs and gilt and shiny red plush.

Burgundy carpet...self-fitting rolls unwinding with precision.

Rusty velvet drapes hanging over exits; resplendent chandeliers; twin masks of Comedy and Tragedy. Everything intimate, well-worn, authentic – except for those reproduction Doric columns which were a structural feature of the store. (One of them, most likely, being the very pillar Bill had earlier leant against.)

And again, as with the notion of people going off to Mass, this thought was comforting.

But it wasn't until a pair of curtains swept across the stage and then – as though only to show themselves in working order, instantly swept back: dusty, maroon curtains with a golden fringe: that I actually realized there *was* a stage; that Odin, Scolopendrid and I were standing on it; and that, without my being aware, the floor of the toy department must have risen up beneath us stripped of all its covering.

Bare boards, however, remained bare for less than a minute. Quite suddenly we found ourselves on grass – on grass, moreover, most shockingly close to the castle. Imagine! Santa's Castle of Snow (formerly of snow) must have come whirling in to form the scenery in much the same way that everything else had come in to form the theatre. The walls and towers and battlements had surely had to be scaled down, but in fact they looked as large as before...and every bit as solid. Even the waters of the moat appeared just as icily forbidding. It seemed that – rather than the castle having got smaller – the stage itself had got bigger. There was still a sense of distance.

Grief! Despite the shock occasioned by a relocating castle, I thought this creation of a theatre comprised a performance the

116

magician might never have surpassed, and, none too surprisingly, he looked as if he would have liked a little praise.

But Odin, now the thing was done, evidently had more on his mind than merely paying compliments. And as the curtains swished apart for the second time – yet on this occasion proved themselves in no great hurry to close – he strode forward and stared across the footlights. By now there was not simply an auditorium. There was an audience.

"Oh, this is diabolical," he crooned. "All those children, all those clean, sweet-smelling children. What a treat they have in store!"

He waved to them welcomingly. As he did so, I heard him say, "Oh, you pesky, pampered, pestilential little creeps." It was pathetic, how trustingly they all waved back.

# 29

"By the stars, in the lie," Mr Scolopendrid had said.

On its own, of course, it was nonsense. Plainly. But on its own it would probably have had to stay. I really hadn't been able to imagine – hadn't been able to *begin* to imagine – how I could ever proceed any further.

Until my dear, good, all-obliging Maurice had decided to impress and entertain his boss by breaking into Latin.

"'Stella'," he had said.

'Stella' meant 'star'. Therefore...something of a waste. I'd already been given it in English.

"'Lux'," he had said.

But I hadn't been given that. Or certainly been given only half of it. Which – in a way – was worse than having been given none at all.

So this could have been a turning point. 'In the lie' was now got rid of. And in its place...

'By the stars, in the light.'

But it still didn't make sense.

117

Yet what it *did* do was remind me of something else that hadn't made sense. I was back in Park Lane. Peering up at the inscription over Odin's door.

Lord Odin's disappearing door.

And, yes, surely...? The mysterious opening words of that inscription...? 'By the Stars, in the Light...'

However, I don't feel I should ever have remembered what came next. Something that rhymed, that was all. I'd been in no fit state on that far-off morning even to understand, let alone absorb.

Yet 'fons' had set me on the right path. Of all those Latin words it was the only one I hadn't recognized. But of all those Latin words it was the only one which kindly Maurice had translated.

*Source!*

Then had come 'vis'. I had known 'vis'.

I had also known 'invenio'.

Known 'utor'.

And it was extra considerate of him even to have arranged them in the right order. Well, more or less the right order. The verbs had come last, of course, but wasn't that where the Romans themselves had liked to place them?

'By the Stars, in the Light, find the Source, use the Strength.'

But no, you idiot, the rhyme...the rhyme! The rhythm. I recalled that even in the midst of my befuddlement, a full three weeks earlier, a part of me had still responded to its lilt.

Might, then. Not strength.

'By the Stars, in the Light, find the Source, use your Might.'

Even now, though, I had no idea of what it meant. But that didn't matter. I was trembling, literally trembling, to think that I'd not only stumbled on the one spell which could bring about the downfall of the enemy – I'd also been presented with the means of putting this knowledge into practice. 'Presented' seemed just about the right word. There were well over fifty children sitting out there in the audience and they had come to me practically gift-wrapped.

And in theory that was all I needed.

Dear heaven... *That was all I needed!*

# 30

"Right," said Odin, turning his back upon the audience and once more facing Scolopendrid. "Now prepare for the contest." In other words: *Bring on the gladiators*! *Where are the lions*?

Odin beckoned me across.

"Rich, old fellow, this is obviously going to be a massacre. But what I'd like you to do is convince those so-called soldiers of the STARS that *they* will be victorious. You see, massacre or no massacre, what everybody wants is a good old-fashioned set-to; not one that will be over in just the twinkling of an eye. Agreed?"

So, acting on this instruction, which anyway accorded with my own wishes, I crossed to the left-hand side of the stage. As I went I felt sick. In my chest I had a trampoline. If there was really going to be a massacre then I was the one entirely to blame. Without question! Earlier, I might have tried to tell myself that something was driving me on – inspiring me, even. But now I realized that this had been naught but wishful thinking.

The troops, all grown to life-size again, were rapidly assembling. Yes, the soldiers of the STARS to the left; the men of Odin to the right. I smiled at the former as they emerged out of the gloom of the department. Some of them even managed to smile back.

Then we huddled together in a corner and watched our foes come tumbling out from under the portcullis, boastfully jostling each other across the drawbridge and delivering many a whooping war cry.

"Look, everybody," I started out by saying – glad that at any rate I could finally jettison pretence and be back amongst my own people. "Odin thinks he's got us licked. But don't be downhearted. *We're* the ones who hold the aces!"

In fact, it was only subterfuge that I had jettisoned, not pretence. But luckily no one asked what these mysterious aces were, and obviously I hoped I could effectively conceal my fear.

However – at least so far as the whirling dervish went – this hope was plainly groundless. He spoke up the second I had finished, and his response began, "Never mind, Mr Semple..." Yes, actually that. *Never mind.*

"Never mind, Mr Semple, I shall throw them all off-course, I shall confuse them, make them giddy. Oh, but how I wish I had a scimitar! Then I'd be a plane propeller – slice, slice, slice! – fingers flying off in all directions. Hands and feet and scalps as well. Yes, really, that could well have kept them at a proper distance!" He sounded wistful. The thought of so much lost opportunity nearly brought him to a standstill.

The ballerina shuddered when she heard him talk this way but only said, "And perhaps I'll be able to confuse them, too: with my pirouettes, my jetés, my steps from Matthew Bourne!" Yet – maybe understandably – she didn't seem all that thoroughly convinced; and my nerves performed some pirouettes and jetés of their own.

"By heaven, *I*...I'm going to bang their silly heads together," promised Esmeralda. "Then, I swear, they'll know what a *tête-à-tête* can truly be! I shall make a bubbling fricassee out of all their brains – such as they have, I mean, which can't be very many."

"And as for me," announced the boxer, "I've got a smashing left hook and a pretty nifty uppercut as well. There'll be a few black eyes, I vow, and loosened teeth and lovely broken jaws before *I'm* through! And I'm banking on at least half-a-dozen good knockouts, too! Our Antipodean friend over there, who clearly fancies himself as a bit of a Cassius Clay...well, let's see how he makes out against somebody his own age, right?"

"And I'll just stand about," suggested the giraffe. "That'll faze 'em. They won't know whether to go round, under, over or what – and then, whichever way they go, I'll simply *swoop* down and nip at the tops of their heads. Or swing them about by the roots of their hair. I promise you, Mr Semple, they won't care very much for *that*."

Oh dear. All this bravery and bravado. Not for the first time this evening there were tears in my eyes but now I wasn't ashamed to have them there – except that, at this point, it certainly wouldn't do for anyone to see them. Because it only required, of course, the executioner with his axe...or the bear, or the boa constrictor, or even the black widow spider...and where would our long-legged, long-necked, hair-pulling friend be then? Him or any of the others?

But straightaway the pirate chief, exactly as if he'd guessed at such pitying and hopeless thoughts, suddenly thumped himself on the chest and gave a cheerful bellow. "Heave ho, my hearties! I'll take on the headsman. I'll have him swimming in the moat; swimming in the moat with his own weighty axe lashed tight at calf and ankle. Pity I can't make him walk the plank and send him down to dine with Davy Jones, but there you are, my beauties – in this life you just have to make the most of what there is – and shiver me timbers if I don't intend to!"

"Yes, tell you what!" exclaimed the footballer, inspired. "We've all got to mark someone; that's the secret of this game. Me, I'll stick close to that gun-toting Mexican bandit. Make sure he doesn't get the chance to fire off a single shot – except, maybe, into a player on his own side." Gratefully he nodded an acknowledgment, both to the whirling dervish and the ballerina. "Thanks, W.D. Thanks, Ludmilla. The name of this game just has to be confusion!"

Twice he had said 'this game'. Looking around me, though, I felt that not many of the contestants had pure sportsmanship in mind.

"Oh, only give me those Barbie dolls," declared Esmeralda. "You can forget about the science! Only give me, please, those two primped and pouting Barbie dolls...and I'll soon make sure they have something very real to pout about!

"Yes, and talking of calf and ankle...," observed the crocodile, reflectively – even if, by now, most of the others had probably forgotten we had been.

But I still felt nauseous. Our foes, now massed on this side of the moat, were laughing raucously; pointing across to us; jeering, whistling; pretending that until the signal could be given they were having to be physically restrained – for such was their impatience to be up and at us!

Then Odin raised his hand. He spoke to *them*, he spoke to *us*, attention equally divided.

121

"Silence, please! I want silence!"

And he got it. Immediately.

"I am about to count to three!"

Distantly, I heard a car or taxi hoot. Oxford Street? The sound was so incongruous, so unreal, it could almost have come from Mars as easily as Marylebone.

"And while I count, you will all remain *exactly* where you are. Not a movement, not a murmur. Until, of course, you hear me get to three. At which point..." He smiled and spread his hands expressively.

Then turned back to the audience.

"Young ladies and gentlemen. Thank you for sitting there so patiently. I hope such patience is going to be most memorably rewarded."

Scolopendrid stepped up to his side.

"Would you like me, Lord, to do the counting?"

"No, thank you, Maurice. Even in my dotage, I think I am still capable of counting up to three."

But something unmistakably significant in the air of his disciple seemed suddenly to make itself felt.

"Oh, very well, if you must! Though, really, all these piddling, pettifogging little details! Then – for pity's sake – don't just stand there. *Count*, why not?"

Scolopendrid obliged; though not before looking back at me, with an air of smug anticipation.

"One!" he proclaimed.

Yes – *smug*. In spite of the Master's sulkiness Maurice was evidently feeling well pleased with himself.

As the resonance of that first numeral died away he looked around importantly. Appeared in no hurry to forsake being at the centre of everyone's unwavering attention.

There followed a pause. A pause of some half-dozen seconds.

"Two!" proclaimed Scolopendrid.

So it seemed I could reckon on having a further six seconds of complete silence.

I was scarcely able to think. My trembling peaked. Went utterly beyond control.

But the '*Two!*' had barely left his lips before I rushed forward and cried out.

Cried out as loudly as I could.

"Children! Quick! Repeat after me! 'By the Stars – '"

*

But why should they obey? They didn't know who I was or what I might be doing. They didn't know that anything was wrong. Why on earth should they obey?

And anyway.

What difference?

Because that was absolutely as far as I could get.

'By the Stars – '

# <u>31</u>

I had forgotten Scolopendrid's arms: how they could stretch. His palm covered my mouth several heartbeats before his face and feet intruded on my vision.

The executioner had also moved fast: leaping over the tussocky, moon-silvered grass, pushing me edgeways and pinioning me with just one hand – *his* arms weren't stretchy but they were sleeveless, thick with muscle. I got shoved down with a jarring thud. My bottom hit the ground, my back hit the side of the proscenium arch. I sat there feeling stunned.

Both he and Scolopendrid had acted out of instinct. Not so their Master. He still stood near the centre of the stage, casting about with steely coldness for something that would suit his purpose. He saw it; snatched the highly-coloured scarf off Esmeralda's shoulders and deftly – but savagely – gagged me with it. "You *idiot*!" he yelled at Scolopendrid.

The white-faced Scolopendrid agreed.

"But, Lord, I'll swear he doesn't – "

"Oh, I'll have you so regretting this!"

"Yes, Master."

"Get rid of those children!"

Up until then I had been too upset and too ashamed to look at the audience – to see its earlier goodwill now turned into bewilderment and consternation; already, perhaps, to downright fear. But when I heard Lord Odin shout out this command there was something else I thought I heard, overlapping his shout.

"Dick!"

Out of all that crazy, disorienting, head-spinning turmoil...something else, that resembled my own name!

"*Dick*! Can you hear me?"

\*

But I'd got to be imagining it. Well, obviously I had.

Because it couldn't be…couldn't conceivably be...just couldn't…?

\*

*Could* it?

Oh dear God, dear God.

I vigorously rub my eyes.

Bill's leaning against that same pillar.

Yes, he's there all right. He's there! It's not a mirage.

Yet this time he's certainly not relaxed. This time...weak? The glow surrounding him barely a glimmer.

"Dick! What have the children got to repeat? I can stave off his power for – possibly – a minute." His voice sounding so strained, so painfully debilitated. "Don't mind about the gag. The gag's irrelevant."

Lord Odin's also heard. Lord Odin isn't quite so steely-calm as he had seemed. "Be gone, be gone!" he cries, running back and forth along the apron of the stage. "Be *gone*, I say!"

Yet it's not so much Bill he appears to be looking at – it's more the children – even though Bill is now speaking to me again. (Why isn't he using *two-way* telepathy?) "It's okay, Dick. Everything's okay. Try to calm down. In a moment you're going to remember it, all of it, the precise wording."

But I can't – I *can't* calm down! Like panicked sheep, my thoughts collide with one another, keep bounding off in all directions.

And I hear another voice.

"It's all right, Lord! I told you. He doesn't know the words!"

I feel that at any moment I may be about to pass out.

"The children!" pleads Bill. "I shan't be able to hold them for very long. And they want so much to help."

I'm beginning to have difficulty in hearing what he says.

"Dick, I know how hard you're trying. Thank you. Thank you for everything. You're really doing a great job."

"Don't you see, Lord? It *is* all right. We're safe!"

The really awful thing is – the absolutely awful thing is – I've got the second bit. 'Find the Strength, use your Might.' But what comes *before* that? 'Might' has to rhyme with something, I know, but with what...dear God, with what? Light? Night? Clearly something to do with the stars – yes, of course – but what? Stars in the night? No, not night. Tight? Right? Fright? Light? All of them rhyme with night – I mean, with might. What else? The sweat is running into my eyes, stinging them and painfully blurring my vision. Oh God, oh God. I can't get it.

Height – sight – light – plight?

It might just as well be Greek – all of it!

(I remember how my mother used to say that. My mum. Suddenly I'm filled with such a longing for her.)

Oh, sweet heaven! That's it! That's it, isn't it?

Not Greek, of course, but Latin!

A mere six words of Latin. So recent, so distinct. And one of them is...one of them is...

*Lux.*

Lux. Meaning light.

*Light*!

Just as I've got it, however...the very second, it seems, that I've managed to effect this breakthrough...

Scolopendrid leans down and puts his hands around my throat.

\*

125

So this, I think, is how it's going to end. Is this really how it's going to end?

Strangely, I'm not frightened. It's more that I'm resigned. Even – no, can this be true? – actually relieved. I think of Harriet and the children. It's practically all over. So in only another minute...in maybe less than another minute...

I suppose it's a pity, though, about the timing; that at the very instant when I'd appeared to be on the verge of coming up trumps...

'By the Stars, in the Light...'

His hands are around my throat but somehow his fingers can't maintain a grip; not so rubbery, after all – they appear to keep on slipping. Yet I'm certain he'll persist. It doesn't really matter. I feel relaxed. Almost sleepy...

Floating... Peaceful...

Something's holding him back, though.

Is it that Bill retains some modicum of power?

Well, if it is...then just let go, Bill. Truly – you can just let go. It doesn't really matter any more.

What do I mean? What do I mean? It doesn't matter any more?

I give a start. Jerk back into wakefulness.

Of course it matters! This isn't only *me*!

"Is that it, Dick? Is that it?" I realize I must have switched off for a moment; I can tell Bill is repeating himself, may have done so more than once. "'By the Stars, in the Light...?'" He's practically gasping.

Shakily I turn my head – my neck sliding easily, despite encircling hands. Even that faint glimmer Bill had been giving off the last time I looked (only *seconds* ago?) is almost gone by now. *Now*, I can scarcely make him out at all.

But he's fighting.

Clearly, he's still fighting.

I remember 1941; that bombed-out building; all that noise and dust and rubble. A steel girder had nearly severed both his legs... "Don't let go," I'd pleaded. "Please don't let go..."

Don't let go, I whisper now. Oh God. I beg it from the very bottom of my heart. Please don't let go.

126

*Please*, God. Don't allow him to let go.

*

But Odin is also a fighter. Odin is also, very much, a fighter.

"Vanish! *Vanish*! *VANISH*!"

Now, though, he's flailing his arms and jumping up and down as if his very bodyweight might somehow shake the place to pieces, send the children catapulting through the crevices, hurl them into outer darkness, every last one of them.

Yet I wouldn't have thought that Bill remained that much of a threat. Can *anybody* understand him? "Children, say it! 'By the Stars, in the Light...'" I suppose, of course, that's what he's trying to tell them.

Scolopendrid has removed his hands from round my neck. I hadn't even noticed.

"I promise you, Lord, I *promise* you: he doesn't know the rest. Don't you remember how you had your eye on me; how you stopped me in the nick of time?"

He adds, with tremendous emphasis, "We – are – going – to – be – all – right!" It's like he's talking to somebody who is very hard of hearing.

But Odin isn't taking any chances. He cries out to his whole frightened army to jump up and down, just like he himself is jumping up and down – to moan and scream and hiss and howl and boo – in short, to make as much noise as they can. Anything; anything. Anything to drown out whatever further words, if any, Bill will desperately try to force up from his strained and spent and unresponsive vocal cords.

"'Find the Strength,'" I think. I think it with all the power and concentration of which I am capable. "'Find the Strength...use your Might.'"

But it's too late. I've left it too late.

Bill has stopped communicating with me.

"'Find the Strength,'" I think. I've just got to get back through to him. I focus every ounce of willpower on trying to get back through to him. Of willpower and sheer bloody-mindedness. "'Find the Strength...use your Might!'" It's partly

127

an injunction to us both. I say it over and over. I can't yet face the fact I've ruined all our chances of success.

Yet still he's gazing at me. Beseechingly. Shaking his head. Is he imploring my forgiveness?

Even his headshake is feeble.

He hasn't got the strength. Not the strength even to shake –

*Not the Strength*! Have I been saying the *Strength*?

The *Source*, not the Strength!

"'Find the Source, use your Might.'" The source – the source – the source! Oh, please, Bill. I know that you can do it. Just hang on in there! Oh, please, God. Help him! Without Bill we're lost. We are all lost.

*I'm* lost, in any case: it's at this point I hear Odin calling to the executioner. "Strike off his head! Just swing that axe, you oaf, strike off his wretched head!" And this time it really means I must be done for. If Bill's energy hasn't totally waned by now he'll be sinking every last vestige into his retransmission of my message.

But all that noise that Odin's men are making!

"Prithee, Master?"

The executioner is cupping his hand to his ear – looks flushed, apologetic – I see it from the corner of my eye. I think: "I'm eighty-three years old and *my* hearing is better than yours!" With his other hand he's still, quite effortlessly, restraining me; ever since the minute I went down – and even through all of Scolopendrid's thwarted bids at strangulation – he's been kneeling there at my side, his axe lying on the ground between us.

Yet the very next instant, also out of the corner of my eye, I see Bill stagger and attempt to save himself. My head swings round and I realize he's now clutching the back of the seat nearest to him...a last futile support, only momentarily delaying his collapse.

But then I see him trying to put his mouth to the ear of a little girl. She strains up towards him.

I see her turn swiftly to the boy beside her...and then that boy turn to his other neighbour...and then...

I see a game of Chinese Whispers.

I remember the wholly ludicrous outcome of every such game I have ever witnessed.

But Scolopendrid has now rushed forward to acquire the axe. He impatiently pushes aside the executioner with a force of which – judging from that lanky, fleshless, runner's frame of his – you mightn't have believed him capable.

I see him raise the axe. He draws it back to take a swing.

Simultaneously, the footballer, the boxer and the pirate chief all dive towards us. There's a fast and furious three-man tackle.

And then the children give a shout. It's barely audible above the ruckus.

But, all the same, it *is* audible.

"'By the Stars, in the Light, find the Source, use your Might.'"

Oh, yes, thank heaven. Thank heaven. Thank heaven.

It *is* audible.

For suddenly there comes a flash of lightning. Just like the ones which struck about an hour ago. But this is a single flash and yet more blinding.

And it is followed by a silence.

Complete silence.

# <u>32</u>

There was, first, the recovery of Bill – whose vitality had been sapped by his responsibility not just for one stupid old man but for a whole theatreful of innocent children. If it hadn't been for Bill, the lives of all those children and of their millions of descendants would have been irreparably affected. No wonder that – having to divide up his strength amongst so many – he had found the experience so extraordinarily debilitating.

There was, next, his overriding priority to reassure those agitated children.

He spoke to them from where he stood.

Then he ran down the gangway and up the few steps that led to the proscenium arch. (By now Esmeralda had removed my gag – *her* gag). He wordlessly threw his arms about me.

After that, with further hugs and gratitude, he turned to Esmeralda herself. Then to all the rest of my team – to every single member of it – although I was scarcely aware of the passage of time. But when we were alone again:

"I knew that you could do it!"

"But I couldn't have. Not without you."

Of course he was hardly able to deny this...even though I felt he might have liked to.

I went on, with mock reproach: "I thought you told me you could never interfere. I thought you claimed it went against the rules."

"Which is perfectly true," he replied. "It does."

"Oh, yeah?" I said.

"Yes, really. We have Odin to thank for my being here. Only Odin."

"Well, naturally. He gave you a complimentary ticket. Said he'd leave it at the box office."

"In a way. Because every time *he* interfered, the rules permitted us to do the same. And in the pressure of the moment – with the gag, for instance – he totally forgot to delegate. So, obviously, there had to be a penalty. All very simple."

He shrugged.

"Or perhaps it wasn't that he forgot. Perhaps he hoped he'd get away with it."

I smiled. I rather supposed that, this time, I might have got him. "You mean...a little like you and the whisky?"

"Now why, I wonder, should you say *that*?"

"I wonder, too."

"Oh, Dick, what a rotten memory you have! Didn't you yourself tell me what happened in Park Lane? Well, up to then how could we have known it was *Odin* who activated the bracelet – as I say, a wanton infringement of the rules? He must have thought he could do it with impunity. Arrogant fellow! But after that, you know, he definitely owed us one."

"The whisky for the manacle? Sounds like a pretty fair trade!

130

By the way, I'd been assured your technology was out of order. How did you know it was Odin who gagged me?"

"Mercifully, we got things mended just in time. Friend Maurice hadn't caused quite the level of damage which he'd inflicted on other occasions. Who knows? He may have had something mildly distracting on his mind – is that a possibility?"

Even so, I gave a shudder.

"So you're telling me that if Odin hadn't slipped up over the bracelet…over the bracelet and the gag...? Because the thing is, Bill, I really believed that I was done for. No hope at all – none! But *then* I discovered my bottle contained only apple juice! And I was instantly reborn! Rose up like the phoenix!"

And if Maurice had actually *tasted* that apple juice, I also thought, instead of merely choosing to wax lyrical about its merry gurgle, its golden lights and amber colouring…! Oh, my!

"Yes, what a crook!" agreed Bill. "Would probably have done quite well in advertising."

I chuckled. "And talk about a message in a bottle! For *that's* when I guessed even the bracelet might have lost its power."

In hindsight, though, there was another way I could have guessed. The bracelet had never recovered its glow – a fact, however, which had no more occurred to me at the time than it could have done to Maurice.

"You touched it with your tears, remember."

"But do you think Odin would have been so fooled? By either the bracelet *or* the apple juice? Incidentally, Bill, what's going to happen to Odin?"

Then I looked about me in alarm. Odin was no longer lying in the place where I had seen him fall.

Bill smiled. "Like me, he's made a very swift recovery."

I felt astonished. Astonished – and even cheated. I glowered. "I thought that this was going to mean the end of him!"

Yet at least I remembered – and almost straightaway – that I no longer had any business to glower; not the least in the world; and when I spoke again I was more reasonable.

"So what have we achieved?"

"Everything," he said. "We have achieved everything! And it took only that one flash of lightning to do it. Celestial lightning," he admitted.

"To do what?"

He shrugged. "Turn him back into the man who had allowed himself to be strung up from an oak tree. Who had allowed one of his eyes to be gouged out – and all in the interests of trying to serve mankind."

I had forgotten that. But I still felt resentful. "A flash of celestial lightning!" I said, sarcastically.

Yet I had to see his point, of course. Reclamation, rather than punishment. "Where is he now?"

Bill gave an ironic nod towards the castle – the real castle, no longer set upon a stage. "Well, they wanted a battle, didn't they?" And indeed it looked as though they might have got their wish. The moon shone down on greensward littered now with heaps of tangled limbs.

And in the heap nearest us I saw that both the Barbie dolls had their legs stuck out at awkward angles. The shadow-boxing adventurer sprawled on his back on top of them. And on top of *him*, Hugin and Mugin were producing only the very feeblest of flutterings.

The bear and the Chinese warlord were floating face downwards in the moat. Someone at that moment was swimming lustily towards them. After a second I saw that it was Odin. Apparently, during the hour following his recovery, and during *just* that hour, it was permissible for Odin to minister to anybody felled by the same lightning flash. To minister himself, that was, without an intermediary.

"And shouldn't *we* be doing something?" I said. After all, the ravens at least were showing signs of life.

"In fact, don't worry, it's not so bad as it looks," Bill reassured me. "They've all had a taste of their own medicine but you'll find they're only stunned – nothing worse. Those twisted limbs can easily be straightened."

Besides, there were already others who were tending to their wounds. Jonathan and Gary were lifting the Mexican bandit onto a stretcher – every bit as carefully as if they had been dealing with a fellow boxer or a fellow footballer. Just ahead of us, Ludmilla was leading by the hand the other Australian, who was still very much dazed, unsteady on his feet, but plainly searching for the friend whom he invariably looked out for. By this time, too, Esmeralda was dragging free the Barbie dolls – Bill said she was meaning to use her busy scarf either as a bandage or a tourniquet, not as a garrotte – and Bearded Black Jack came stumbling behind us with the executioner slung mute across his shoulder. It really did look as though I wasn't needed.

Wrong, though. Somewhere, I *was* needed...and pretty speedily, at that! Mr Scolopendrid – our friend, Maurice the Magical, "how the kiddies all love me!" – had been largely overlooked.

Overlooked, that is, by everyone except the crocodile. Limpopo, indeed, was now overlooking him with the keenest possible interest: inspecting his ankles, in particular, with the pursed-up lips of one who was known to be quite an authority on such a subject.

Actually, I should have said, only a short time back, I'd feel no compassion whatsoever for the ankles of Mr Maurice Scolopendrid.

But then I noticed Odin moving backwards from the moat and dragging the warlord up the muddy bank to safety (in fact, to the same grassy spot where the rescued bear was still recovering) and this, added to the current example of my loyal team-mates, must have produced a somewhat softening effect.

"Anyway, there's not much meat on those ankles, or even on those calves," I told the disappointed crocodile, who stared up at me reprovingly and looked as though he could have kicked himself for forgetting an age-old adage: *he who hesitates is lost.* "However, I'll tell you what we'll do. I think for better or worse we'll make him a little gift of my crystal ball." (Which now took me scarcely three seconds to detach from around my waist.)

In the meanwhile I tickled the crocodile's tummy...it seemed to compensate for his having felt hard-done-by. I told him the world wasn't a fair place. He appeared gradually to accept this. Shortly, he had acquired much the same soppy air of ecstacy as Bombles.

133

Odin now came striding across. No longer looking like a male model being photographed for *Esquire* or *GQ* – not right at the moment, anyway – he was nevertheless a good advertisement for the curative properties of lightning. Tentatively, he held out his hand.

"I hope, Mr Semple, that one day you'll be able to find it in your heart to forgive me."

Almost automatically I held out my own hand – and at once despised myself for doing so. I did *not* mean to appear forgiving. Neither forgiving nor friendly.

He said: "I'd also like to ask your forgiveness on behalf of all my henchmen; although not one of them, of course, is a hundredth part to blame as much as I."

("Limpopo!" I had to exclaim, warningly. I suppose it wasn't *too* unnatural that he should have this hang-up over ankles.)

"And, lastly, before we part" – Odin must have realized I drew scant pleasure from his company – "I want to thank you for my freedom; for the end to all those centuries of incarceration!"

"That's okay," I growled. Because, after all, how else *can* you reply when someone wants to thank you for terminating countless centuries of incarceration?

"The seal is broken – never again shall I need to spend time in my fortress of fear!"

"I'm glad, Lord Odin."

"Only Odin," he corrected me, a little sadly. "Only Odin."

And actually it suddenly occurred to me that I had almost meant what I said. (And I somehow decided, at nearly that same moment, not to lumber Scolopendrid with the crystal ball. In fact…couldn't I just hang onto it myself? Hadn't what-might-have-been unexpectedly become what's-going-to-be?)

He shook my hand again; then walked off, tactfully, when he saw that Bill was coming back.

I wasn't too keen, though, for Bill to read the muddled state of my reflections. I swiftly put another question.

"No, you mustn't fret!" he said. (And it was true: I *had* been fretting over this.) "W.D. – Ludmilla – the Barbie dolls – Black Jack – the two adventurers: *everyone* is going to find a good home." When Bill glanced at the audience his look was clearly optimistic. "I think, in fact, we should be able to do some quite excellent marrying-up."

Zarafah, even as Bill told me this, was gazing down curiously on both of us. I reached up to stroke his long neck; he instantly lowered it. I wondered if by now he'd got used to being life-sized, and whether he would mind having to return to something a good deal smaller.

I also wondered which family *he* might choose to go to when the time came and whether there'd be any opportunity to go on seeing him – along with all the others I had grown attached to.

*

Almost the very first question I had asked:

"And what about the children, Bill? I mean…who *are* those children, anyway, and where on earth have they come from?"

"They've come from San Francisco."

"*Really?*"

"Yes, really. You see, at roughly half-past-three this afternoon, *their* time, which is nine hours behind London, they were all sitting with their families in the Orpheum Theatre, watching *Peter Pan*. Totally in thrall to its magic. 'If you believe in fairies,' they were told, 'you must now clap like you've never in all your lives clapped for anything before!' Well, naturally, they threw their whole hearts into it. The grown-ups smiled and played along…though not at all as if anyone's existence might actually depend on it."

Bill himself smiled.

"But that didn't matter. There were enough children there to save Tinker Bell. Yet here's the thing, Dick…their desperate clapping just happened to coincide with a downpour of petals, carnation petals, five thousand miles or so to the east. And this applause was like a whirlwind stirring up a multitude of runes. Stirring them in such a way as to draw the very spirits out of those clapping children and waft them from one theatre full of enchantment into another – one newly constructed but by chance plugged into the same frequency."

"Albeit, for a very different purpose," I commented, dryly.

135

"Yes, but runes, remember – as Odin realized only too well in the old days and will quickly rediscover now – runes don't distinguish between the powers of good and evil."

"But, anyway, what about the children's parents? Don't tell me they haven't even noticed!"

"That they're not worrying, you mean, because their kids seem suddenly so drowsy? Why, even as we speak, the reason's being attributed either to too many late nights – or else to too big a lunch at McDonald's!"

He smiled again.

"No, Dick, if the *families* aren't alarmed, why should you be? For – take my word – the spirits will be wafted back in time for every child to clap wildly at the end of *Peter Pan*. They may not know quite why they're feeling so happy...but happy they'll most certainly be. In fact, they'll think it's because of the toy they've just discovered in their laps: the very toy they'd already lost their hearts to in London, had they but known it. Everyone, adults and children alike, will imagine it's a present from the management – though how, in the name of everything that's holy, did the management ever pull off such a stunt: a special effect, and a special delivery, more mystifying than anything occurring on the stage?"

He grinned.

"But, anyway, Dick, these children will soon be experiencing a treat which will banish utterly and for all time any lingering impression of nastiness. A treat which they'll remember all their lives...even though, of course, they'll always stay convinced they only dreamt it."

\*

Bill said: "And talk about some excellent marrying-up... In the circumstances, we feel it's not unreasonable to make another small exception."

*Small* exception? A man and two women came walking swiftly from the wings. They looked in their mid-twenties and could easily have been mistaken for brother and sisters. Yet somehow I knew them – knew them on the instant. And if anything gave me a single moment's pause it was nothing but the sheer incredible magnificence of it all.

"Harriet! Oh, my God. Harriet. And Pete. And Naomi. I...I... You really shouldn't touch me; I'll only make you dirty."

"Oh, my darling! As if touching you could ever make us dirty."

"Dad, you old fox. You did it! You really did it."

"At school, Daddy, we always boasted you could take on anyone. And now you see how very *right* we were!"

"And had you only known," Bill said to Naomi, "you could then have boasted St Nicholas himself would one day want to shake your father's hand."

"Oh, darn it!" she laughed. "Can we all go back?"

"And that, just in order to do so, he would make an extended stopover in London."

What's more, scarcely had Bill said this before I thought I heard the sounds of arrival. In Bill's world – and I had to remind myself, in Harriet's and Peter's and Naomi's, as well – it appeared that things were very carefully timed. They happened pretty much on cue.

But wouldn't you have thought St Nicholas would arrive by sleigh?

And even if on foot...well, with a somewhat heavier and more stately kind of tread?

Not running.

Nor in boots that seemed to be hitting the floorboards with a rhythmic slap. A sort of soft and muffled slap, like fluffy mules.

Nor calling out my name in a voice which sounded like a woman's and had an unmistakably Cockney accent.

No, indeed. I had to think again.

*St Nicholas?*

Well, obviously his timing wasn't *quite* so spot-on as I'd just been giving him credit for.

# 33

"Oh, Mr Semple, Mr Semple. You're never going to believe this. All I meant to do was rest my eyes for a jiffy – get a second wind, like. And that was *four hours* ago! You can't imagine how *guilty* I feel!"

She looked about as guilty as an athlete taking gold at the Olympics.

"Though I've had such lovely dreams! Dreamt I was a star, exactly like I told you I'd always wanted to be – remember? Oh, well, never mind *that*. But I also dreamed about you, Mr Semple; and there was this young lady in the dream – she sounded posh but ever so nice – and she was urging me to give old Fred a call. So, the minute I woke up, I did. And what do you think he said? 'Oh, go on then, he can stay.' Just like that: no ifs and buts: nothing. *Oh, he can stay, then, if he wants to!*"

She stopped at last, and simply gazed at me, eyes shining, hands clasped.

"That's very kind," I faltered. I felt a bit perplexed. "But before you say another word, let me introduce you to my wife and children – and my friends."

Bill, however, shook his head.

"No, Dick, she can't see us. She can't see or hear anybody on this stage, other than you and Maurice Scolopendrid." (Perhaps it was as well she hadn't caught sight of *him* yet.) "As a matter of fact, she doesn't even realize that it *is* a stage."

Oddly enough, Rita Whipplecrump now shook her head as well, almost in unison. "Oh, you poor dear. You've also been asleep, haven't you? You've also been having some smashing dreams. Oh, why did I have to go and wake you up? Rushing in like that, in all my excitement!"

She could hardly have woken me up; I was very much upon my feet. It was like  when Bill had taken me across to Blitzen, then soon afterwards disappeared, and I had wondered, with almost a sense of bereavement, if I'd merely been asleep.

"But, Mrs Whipplecrump," I said, "I appreciate your rushing in like that, in all your excitement."

"And no wonder, then, you haven't touched your Christmas dinner. Well, who cares about that, any more? There'll be a nice pot of soup on the stove – bound to be. He has his uses, my old Fred."

She laughed, affectionately.

"So, of course, *that's* why I went and woke you up. It's high time we were setting off. High time for both of us to be getting our skates on!"

But I didn't want to leave just yet.

Though how could I explain?

"And to get home all the quicker," she said, "I've decided to treat us to a taxi! Makes it more special, like. Must be something in the air... You know what, Mr Semple? It suddenly feels like Christmas!"

I chuckled.

"I thought that, for you, it felt like Christmas earlier. Or had you forgotten?" I even took a shot at singing the opening words of it myself. "'Rudolf the red-nosed reindeer... had a very shiny nose...'"

"Oh, well," she laughed, "but that was different. All that was, that was just trying to keep our spirits up, weren't it? And what a great success that was – I *don't* think! Not like you dreaming about your wife and family."

"I'm sorry I was rude to you."

"Oh, gracious, no need to apologize for that. Up to now, life hasn't exactly been a picnic, has it? But, from here on, we're going to bust our flipping garters, aren't we, just to make sure it turns into one? Okay? You up for that?"

"It already has," I smiled. "Turned into a picnic. Dear God, how it already has!" Harriet had long since slipped her hand into mine and was resting her head against my arm. Naomi had hold of my other hand and Peter was standing behind me, giving my shoulder a reassuring squeeze.

I suppose it should have felt *especially* strange about the children. At the time of the accident they had both been so very young, only seven and eight, for heaven's sake! Now, just like their mother, they were in their prime – as Bill had promised me they would be. Radiant and in their prime.

139

But no, it didn't feel in the least bit strange.

Surprisingly, too, I wasn't frustrated at being unable to talk to them. It was enough simply to have all three so close. I had no sense of Rita being an intruder.

I told her of the upcoming arrival of St Nicholas.

And it wasn't difficult to read her expression. One of us, it clearly said, was still drifting very happily in and out of dreamland.

But I needn't have worried about explanations: suddenly, a brilliant shaft of light was falling across the department and countless cowbells – or, at any rate, *bells* – could now be heard ringing.

I have a small problem here, however. Although I'd like to be a bit more precise about how St Nicholas actually entered the premises of Hagalaz & Son, and to record my observations in minute and scientific detail...albeit, of course, in language still accessible to the common man...well, the fact of the matter is...

He just sort of materialized through the ceiling.

Sitting in his sleigh.

And he wasn't quite what I'd expected!

Of course, one gets so used to seeing Santa in the sort of traditional garb I myself was in part wearing: with scarlet hood framing an old man's face – usually a kind and humorous face, all rosy cheeks and jovial grin – but, nonetheless, still that of an *old* man. White hair, white beard, wrinkles. The lot.

But naturally I should have realized. Didn't I have before me the prototypes of Bill and Harriet, Peter and Naomi? Even of Odin? So why had I thought it would be any different for St Nicholas? Seventeen hundred years or not, I mean, since his days of being a bishop in Asia Minor?

After all, hadn't he and Odin been contemporaries? I imagine they could even have met.

Might well have attended the same cocktail parties!

You see, what I'm saying is this. The person before me looked somewhere between the ages of twenty-eight and thirty-five, clean-shaven, dark-haired, brown-eyed. He wore a black bubble coat, jeans and white trainers. (But then, in fact, I saw his Santa costume tucked beneath his seat.) And as he stepped down

140

from the sleigh, he looked fit, happy, unassuming – with the kind of glow Bill and my family possessed and which in some strange way remained brilliant, even in the midst of brilliance.

Yes, there he was, standing right before us, like some particularly smiley ambassador. I half wondered if I should go down on my knees...although without making such a parade of it as certain others, or one certain other, had recently been known to do. But I didn't. I felt St Nicholas wouldn't be the kind to want to stand on ceremony.

So then...

But in the way I can't *quite* describe his manner of entry into the building, it's also hard remembering the order in which things occurred after his arrival. I'm tempted to say they all occurred at the same time. But I strongly suspect that this too, printed in the pages of the *New Scientist*, might sound just a little...well, questionable.

Anyhow, here are some of those occurrences.

Blitzen...

With whoops of delight, St Nicholas greeted Blitzen. He hugged him and then took pleasure in watching him reunite with his siblings.

Myself...

To begin with, he beckoned me forward and shook my hand. Then, placing his hands upon my shoulders, he began to extol my 'truly devastating' achievement. ("Oh, no, it was nothing," I said, "please don't mention it...anybody could have done it." "Ah, yes, the typically modest Englishman!" he laughed. "Shouldn't I have guessed?" Ironically, as he said this, I noticed his accent and speech rhythms, which reminded me *he* wasn't an Englishman, not at all.) And while he was talking I grew aware of how compelling I found him and of how much I hoped I might one day get to know him.

Odin...

I saw him give Odin a slap on the back and without the slightest hint of recrimination, or even of forgiveness, heard him float the possibility of their working together in the future.

"Oh, it's so good to see you again!" he said excitedly – as if the slightly bashful man who now stood before him in his soaked

141

and muddy lounge suit, with his bright blue eye uncharacteristically cast down, had been returning from a world cruise that could perhaps have lasted over centuries…and as if this was the moment of their reunion on the dockside.

Mrs Whipplecrump…

St Nicholas conferred on Rita – although, I need scarcely add, without any kind of condescension – a favour of a different sort: he arranged it so that she could see him. Then he asked after Fred's arthritis, and about her mother's ongoing progress following an illness in the summer, and commended Rita on her positive approach to all the many difficulties she had to face. "We're all in the gutter," he smiled, "but some of us are looking up at the stars. Right? Platitudinous, but right?" He gave her a friendly grin, and clasped her hand briefly, before reluctantly turning away.

Perhaps Scolopendrid was next in line, who knows? Obviously, by this time, Rita had realized he was there. "Oh, look," she had gasped, "old Meanypants! Oh, Mr Semple. You don't think he could have *heard* me, do you?" But the knowledge that his fifth-floor cleaner had dropped off for a few hours, owing to sheer exhaustion, wasn't something old Meanypants now seemed so likely to dwell upon – not, that is, in the current grand scheme of things. For St Nicholas was talking to him, man-to-man, about the pleasures open to the very rich, of being able to scatter a few of their pennies amongst the very poor.

Well, indeed, he was being a little more specific than that.

"Maurice, we all know how at Christmas you've always taken the greatest interest in your toy department. Which presumably indicates a wish to put big smiles onto the wistful faces of the young? Therefore, what about donating a few of your pennies to those who work to do precisely that? NSPCC, Gingerbread, Children in Need, Barnardo's…"

"A few of my pennies…?" inquired the potential smile-provider; a shade uncertainly.

Whereupon St Nicholas made a suggestion which, for some reason, gave rise to a bit of a stutter.

"Doh…doh…doh…donate a million pounds?"

"No, no, no," laughed St Nicholas, merrily; evidently enjoying their small misunderstanding. "Dear Maurice, forgive me – my fault – I was clearly being a mite ambiguous! Did you think I meant a million divided up between the four? Oh, dear me, no. What I meant was a million pounds *each*. Well, just to begin with," he smiled, encouragingly.

Up until then I'd been vaguely wondering whether Mr Scolopendrid had received the same treatment-by-lightning as Lord Odin. But from his unaltered style of conversation and ultra-sickly smile, I judged that *he*, at any rate, hadn't so far been given the full monty. I judged that Mr Scolopendrid had yet to be reformed.

On the other hand, I got the feeling it might still be thought a possibility.

"No lengthy waiting lists," promised St Nicholas. "This isn't the NHS."

*

St Nicholas also spoke to all the children in the audience – yes, and every single one of them looked wide-eyed and enraptured.

But what next?

Well...

He presented me with a parcel wrapped in brown paper, containing an old and crumpled manuscript, instantly recognizable as a story I'd written long ago for my two children. *Two on a Tiger*.

There was a card inside the cover.

> *Dearest Richard,*
> *Thank you for making this such a very special Christmas –*
> *for everybody, everywhere!*
> *With my warm affection and abiding gratitude,*
> *Nick.*

Along with the manuscript, the parcel contained a second package: the photograph and mementoes I thought I'd lost forever; my spectacles and cutlery and UB40. There was also a most generous cheque made out to me by Odin – well, no, it was actually Salmonica Longspoon whose signature appeared on it – but it was he who had scribbled the few covering lines. "I realize nothing can compensate for all the unpleasantness I've recently put you through, but hope you'll accept the enclosed as a small token of my appreciation and regard. Again, my most fervent and humble apologies. Odin." It seemed fresh evidence of his being a completely remodelled character. Furthermore, in view of how he'd got the cheque to me so fast, along with my once-lost possessions, it seemed fresh evidence that he and old Merlin could still be members of the same club.

*

We didn't follow Rita's suggestion of a taxi; although she later, pretty weirdly, believed we had; and not missing any of her own money, she repeatedly declared *I* must have paid for the cab – which I most certainly would have, if we had actually taken one! She kept trying to push a twenty-pound note into my pocket, having said at least twice that she hoped this would take care of the tip as well as the journey.

But, in fact, I don't think reindeer care a lot about tips.

Because *that*, you see, is how we'd got there: to Rita's home.

No taxi, no taxi driver. Just eight happy reindeer, cheerfully harnessed to the sleigh which St Nicholas – well, *Nick*, as he'd invited me to call him – had absolutely insisted we should borrow. For in his own special time zone, he'd assured us, the world's presents would still get very punctually delivered.

(And even when he'd said this…by then it must have been well after two a.m. Greenwich Mean Time.)

We'd enjoyed a brilliant ride and despite the lack of a control tower in Balfour Street a brilliant touchdown. The best landing you could possibly have hoped for.

Or almost so. There was maybe one small thing lacking

You see, every house except Rita's happened to be in darkness. So this meant there wasn't a single human being to witness our arrival…only a couple of companionable cats, who gave over grooming themselves for a while.

144

Yet all the same...

"Here," suggested Rita, "why don't we set off a few car alarms up and down the road? We *can't* waste such a smashing opportunity as this! We've got to keep up with the Joneses – got to get our picture in the paper! My mum would be so proud."

Yet, sadly, we were forced to waste it, that smashing opportunity. And more sadly still, we soon found ourselves having to say goodbye to Blitzen – to Blitzen and his seven siblings. We watched them climb back into the heavens and waved forlornly till they'd disappeared.

Fred came to the front door of No 22. He was short and wiry. Walked with an obvious limp.

"You paid off the taxi, then?" he said to his wife.

"Dick did." He and I were introduced. He gave me a brusque nod.

For the minute, though, Rita seemed reluctant to go inside. She stood in the road and gazed wistfully beyond the rooftops.

"Here, did you ever hear this?" she said. "'We're all in the gutter but some of us are looking at the stars.'"

"Or reading them in the *Evening Standard*, more like!" replied Fred. "Come on, Mrs Nostradamus! There's mulligatawny on the stove."

He then retreated into the house. His wife shrugged and pulled a face. "He's right, you know, Mr Semple." (Force of habit: she'd soon get back to calling me Dick.) "Bit too cold for stargazing! Can't think what got into me!"

Then she gave me a closer look and her returning smile grew broader. "Nor into you, neither!"

Because for one magical moment my own gaze had once again been drawn up, irresistibly, into that clear and moonlit sky, with its frosty and diamond-bright constellations, and my silly old eyes had once again grown watery as I'd said a few silent words of love and thanks to Harriet and my children – and to Bill, as well; and had somehow been reassured that the rest of my life was going to be just wonderful.

"It's Christmas," I said.

"Yes," said Rita. "It's Christmas... Happy Christmas, Mr Semple!"